AMBUSH

Hatfield had been riding a little too long, and he needed sleep and food as badly as he ever had. When he saw the line camp of the Rafter B in the distance, he relaxed and allowed the tiredness to flow through him; he was there.

As he rode up to the shack, he saw the Mexican waiting for him. "Como 'sta? You Pancho?" he asked the man assigned to help him.

The vaquero nodded, then said, "Put bedroll inside. I take you up-canyon to Marsh."

Hatfield dismounted and began to move. It came at him so quickly, he wasn't conscious of Pancho's gun butt driving into his head . . . of a second man pointing a six-gun at his heart.

THE TOMBSTONE TRAIL

JACKSON COLE

isbn 978-1-64720-201-9

Fiction House Press
www.FictionHousePress.com

CHAPTER I

Texas Manhunter

A howling Texas norther drove its oblique lash of rain across the Big Bend, through which the lighted windows of the Chisos relay station loomed mistily, like a cougar's eyes reflected in a campfire's sheen. Occasional lightning flashes revealed pinched-off glimpses of the Rosillo Mountain foot slopes with the frowning peaks of the Corazones rearing above the storm.

The wet gale sweeping toward Mexico set the mesquites and cholla cactus to plunging like stampeded animals. Off beyond the Chisos stock tender's corral, flood waters made their angry muttering between the shale cutbanks of Tornillo Creek, rushing in unbridled flood toward the Rio Grande.

Down the ribbon of mud which followed the old Spanish route of conquest, the weekly Wells-Fargo stagecoach was slogging along the second leg of its Marfa to Alpine to Presidio run. Its oil lamps appeared as a pair of nimbus-circled yellow blurs swimming through this drowned night.

The Chisos hostler spotted the oncoming lights and, with a curse for the storm's fury, donned his overcoat and headed for his adobe barn to harness a fresh span of Morgans. This night was at the mercy of the elements. West Texas inhabitants would date future events from this torrential downpour.

On the crest of the mud-sloppy hogback overlooking the way station, two men in oilskin slickers and tall sombreros emerged from the chaparral and saw the lights of the approaching stage. One of the pair hastened his steps, while his companion drew back instinctively on the handcuff which linked them wrist to wrist.

Down the slope they came, limping from the torture of tight-fitting spike-heeled cowboots which were not designed for walking. Like black ghosts they reached the Tornillo Creek flats and followed the corral fence along the stage road toward the depot.

The Wells-Fargo Concord was having heavy going, its high wheels stoppered with gluelike adobe mire. So the handcuffed pair reached the station five minutes ahead of the plodding vehicle.

Mike Conroy, the stock tender, emerged from his *aguista*-roofed barn with six harnessed Morgans, led them under the dripping shelter of the depot awning. He saw the two men in oilskins standing by the door, and the sight of them brought an astonished oath to Conroy's whisker-screened mouth.

"Jim Hatfield!" the stock tender cried. "Captured Radley, eh? I thought you two would shoot it out back in Paisano Pass."

The fanwise slant of light from inside the station revealed the fatigue-rutted, stubbled face of the man Conroy had addressed as Jim Hatfield. The light also glinted off the steel fetters which manacled him to his brutish-faced companion.

"Time for a cup of java before the stage leaves, Mike?" Hatfield inquired wearily.

"Yeah. Go inside and tell my missus to feed yuh. Texas Rangers don't pay for grub at my place, Hatfield."

Hatfield led his prisoner into the warmth of Conroy's lunch room. As the door closed behind them, the stagecoach pulled off the army road and lumbered to a halt under the depot's shelter.

Before Zeke Bledsoe, the jehu, had time to climb down from the boot, Mike Conroy had unhooked the tug straps and was leading the jaded team toward the barn. Bledsoe, looking like a drowned rat in his slicker and battered sombrero, opened the door of the Concord and addressed his passengers inside.

"Half-hour's stop here, folks," he said. "Hot coffee and sandwiches inside. Last chance to get a snack of bait before we hit the Rio."

Two passengers alighted stiffly from the thoroughbraced coach—a pot-bellied drummer representing a cowboy bootery in Denver, who had boarded the stage at Alpine yesterday, and a slim, rosy-cheeked girl wearing an aigrette-feathered hat, form-fitting bodice and gray marseilles skirt. She was around twenty, Bledsoe judged. She had paid her fare through to Alto, over in Thundergust Basin, when she had boarded his stage at Fort Davis.

The drummer took the girl's arm and escorted her inside the stage depot. Mike Conroy's wife was busy waiting on the two slicker-clad men who had waded in out of the night. Bledsoe was checking the grease in a hind wheel hub when Mike Conroy got back from the barn and backed the fresh team alongside the tongue of the Concord.

"Couple more passengers waitin' inside, Zeke," Conroy told the jehu. "Big folks. The Lone Wolf Texas Ranger, Jim Hatfield, and a smuggler he dabbed his loop on back in the hills—Les Radley."

As much as old Zeke Bledsoe needed hot coffee and a chance to let warmth soak into his bones, he was stopped in his tracks by the stock tender's news.

"The dickens yuh say! How'd that Ranger ever locate Radley? Posses have been combin' the Big Bend for that Border-hopper for over a year, now."

Conroy, whose lonely existence was seldom enlivened by such high drama as this, looked up from his job of harnessing the team to the waiting coach.

"Hatfield got off the stage here last Monday. Seems the Rangers got a tip-off that Radley was hidin' at a sheep camp up on Paisano Pass. Hatfield took out for the Pass on foot, and I never figgered I'd see him alive ag'in. But he's in there now—bagged his meat."

The stage tooler waggled his head in amazement as he walked into the warmth of the stage station and sat down at the lunch counter. Jim Hatfield and Les Radley occupied stools at the far end of the counter, drinking their coffee in silence. Puddles of rain water had drained off their slickers to muddy the floor.

Handcuffed wrist to wrist, they appeared like twins in their identical garb. Both were men of better than average height and bulk. Their faces showed the strains of a twenty-mile trek out of the mountains, and their jaws were furred with stubble.

When Mrs. Conroy had brought the driver his order, old Zeke took his plate and tin cup over to where his girl passenger sat beside the porcine-jowled drummer. Obviously bored by the fat man's efforts to engage her in conversation, the girl turned eagerly to old Bedloe, who seized avidly at his opportunity to divulge a juicy morsel of rangeland gossip.

"See them hard cases yonder?" the jehu whispered, gesturing toward the handcuffed pair with his sugar spoon. "Most famous men in the Lone Star State. Yuh'll share the stage with 'em tonight."

Beth Beloud—which was the name old Zeke had spotted on the alligator bandbox he had stowed in the canvas-curtained compartment behind the Concord—twisted her head to stare at the slicker-clad duo at the far end of the counter. Both men were eating greedily, their rutted faces showing their fatigue as they crouched in moody silence.

"So?" the girl answered politely. "Who are they?"

Zeke Bledsoe leaned closer, his voice low and confidential.

"Jim Hatfield, the Ranger they call the Lone Wolf," he said. "Best star toter in the Rio Grande country. His prisoner is Les Radley, one of them Tombstone Trail smugglers. Killer-lobo, Radley is. It's a wonder to me how Hatfield captured him alive. There's a five-thousand-buck reward on Radley's topknot."

Conroy stuck his head in the door at that moment, a blast of moist wind causing the lamps to gutter violently.

"Rider just got in from the Rio, Zeke. Says the flood's risin' fast in the Tornillo, and is li'ble to wash out the bridge downriver if yuh don't pull out of here pronto."

Zeke bolted his food and left the counter, walking over to where the Ranger and his prisoner sat.

"Yuh heard what he said, gents," Bledsoe said. "If yu're leavin' on my stage, settle up with Missus Conroy and come along. If that bridge washes out we'll be marooned on this side of the creek for a week."

Further down the counter, the moon-faced drummer laid a hand on Beth Beloud's wrist familiarly.

"I'm packin' a gun, ma'am," he whispered unctuously. "Don't you worry about bein' cooped up in the same stage with a desperado. I'll see that no harm comes to yuh tonight."

Beth smiled faintly. Throughout this storm-lashed day, the boot salesman had tried to talk with her. She had found his overtures mildly obnoxious. The fat man was of a predatory breed common to the frontier.

"Thanks," she said drily. "Which is which? I can't pick out the Ranger from the bad man."

Radley and the Texas Ranger were heading for the door, their slickers rustling, the link of the handcuff making its metallic jingle between their wrists.

The drummer, knowing the famous Lone Wolf Ranger only by repute, swelled expansively and leaned over to put his flabby lips close to the girl's ear.

"The one on the left is Jim Hatfield," he whispered. "The other one is the Tombstone Trail smuggler. Yuh'll never see a more dangerous man than Radley, ma'am. He's responsible for some of them graves that give Tombstone Trail its name, and yuh can bank on that."

Beth Beloud left a coin on Mrs. Conroy's counter—which paid for the drummer's food as well as her own—and permitted the pudgy salesman to escort her back outdoors.

The rain had doubled in violence. Standing alongside the wheelers, Zeke Bledsoe was engaged in conversation with a raw-boned cowboy in a sopping wet brush-popper jumper who had just ridden in out of the storm.

"Make shore the bridge is safe before yuh try to cross," Beth heard the cowboy warn the jehu. "There's been a cloudburst upriver and this flash flood is workin' on the trestle. My bronc bucked like a tornado before I could lead him across. Animals have a way of knowin' when a bridge ain't safe."

Mike Conroy opened the stage door and stood to one side as the drummer and Beth Beloud stepped inside. Jim Hatfield and his prisoner had taken the front seat, riding backward to the course of the stage, thereby leaving the favored seat for the girl and her self-appointed escort.

A light glowed inside the Concord and Beth Beloud snuggling her hands into a fur muff while the courtly drummer arranged a laprobe across her knees, took advantage of the moment's delay to study the grim-faced pair seated opposite.

Born and raised in Texas, she had heard of Jim Hatfield. His name was as familiar to her as a lawman as Les Radley's was notorious as an outlaw. Now, eyeing them covertly, she was surprised to see that the Lone Wolf had a furtive, predatory face, whereas Radley, the outlaw, was a man whose rugged good looks struck a chord of admiration in the girl, in spite of herself.

It did not occur to her that the drummer had possibly mixed up his identification of the pair, in his eagerness to impress her with his own knowledge of rangeland celebrities. But such had been the case. So far as Beth knew, she would never see again this oddly contrasted pair of men when their stage reached its destination and their paths separated. And she had no way of knowing that the drummer had switched identities.

Outside, Zeke Bedloe's whip popped against the roar of the storm and the Morgans lunged into their collars. The Concord jounced violently on its bullhide thoroughbraces, and the lights of Mike Conroy's lonely station dropped behind the pelting rain.

And Death rode this Wells-Fargo stage tonight. Behind the cover of the torrential downpour, it waited on black wings, poised to strike, waiting for the appointed hour as written in The Book.

CHAPTER II

Death Strikes

For Jim Hatfield, this stagecoach run to the Rio Grande and thence up to district headquarters at Presidio marked the end of a manhunt which had engaged the energies of the Texas Rangers for better than five years.

Les Radley, the sullen, heavy-jawed outlaw who sat at his left rubbing knees with the drummer in front of him, was a *contrabandista* who for more than a decade had plied his illicit business of smuggling drugs, aliens and 'dobe dollars out of Mexico. He was a high-ranking member of that legion of rock-eyed Border-hoppers who employed the historic "Tombstone Trail" as their smuggling route.

Tombstone Trail had originally been an old Aztec artery of commerce, coming from the southern *cordilleras* of Hidalgo and leading across Texas' Big Bend, the Staked Plain, and winding up in the Indian Nations. Spanish *conquistadores* had traveled the trail northward in the 1500s, in search of the fabulous Seven Cities of Cibola. Smugglers and other men outside the law had used it in more recent times. It derived its sinister name from the number of unmarked graves which stood like milestones along its tenuous route.

When the pressure of Chihuahua *Rurale* Police and The U.S. Border Patrol had made Tombstone Trail's ford on the Rio Grande untenable for smuggling operations, Les Radley had vanished. But a small-time member of the Tombstone Trail gang, who had recently been arrested by Jim Hatfield in El Paso, had tipped off the Texas Ranger that Radley could most likely be found in hiding in Paisano Pass.

Captain Bill McDowell, of the Austin headquarters, had assigned his top-ranking Ranger, Jim Hatfield, to invade Radley's hideout. "Roaring Bill" wanted Radley captured alive, as a possible means of learning where the smuggler ring had its headquarters, and the identity of its chief.

The famous Lone Wolf had done his job well. Now he he was talking Les Radley to district headquarters in Presidio.

He had run a desperate risk in capturing Radley alive; but Hatfield was looking ahead to wiping out the entire Tombstone Trail contraband traffic, and he knew that Radley, behind bars, might prove a valuable source of information which would lead to the arrest of his chief, and other henchmen whose identities were not yet known to the law.

Intermittent flashes of lightning filtered through the canvas window curtains of the lumbering Concord and revealed to Hatfield that he was the subject of a discreet appraisal by the pretty black-haired girl seated opposite him. He was struck by her beauty, and wondered vaguely what she was doing in this uncurried back of beyond, wondered if she were married to the gross man in city clothing who shared the back seat with her.

Outside, Zeke Bledsoe reined his team to a halt and set his foot brake. Climbing down over the front wheel, the old Wells-Fargo tooler walked out on a narrow plank bridge which spanned the Tornillo Creek canyon.

Swinging his lantern out over the rushing waters, Bledsoe shuddered at the unleashed fury of the churning current below. The Tornillo was running nearly bank high, its muddy flow choked with brush and uprooted trees which were beginning to jam against the heavy piers of the bridge.

As the rider had warned him back at the Chisos station, five miles upstream, this bridge was in imminent danger of being washed out. Such a calamity was to be avoided at all costs, for Bledsoe knew that another bridge, twenty miles north, would be out before he could get back to it.

Inspecting the bridge carefully, feeling the shudder of its underpinnings as the foaming current boiled down between the lava rimrocks, Bledsoe decided to take the long chance. The bridge was only forty feet long. It would surely hold up under the weight of his six-horse team and the comparatively light Concord.

Going back to his perch on the hurricane deck, Bledsoe set his lantern in its bracket and unwound his lines from the Jacob's staff. A veteran reinsman, with more than twenty years' experience on this Fort Davis-Rio Grande run, Bledsoe had seen this bridge hold up under freshests in the past. He believed it was safe now, and therefore elected not to put his four passengers to the inconvenience of getting out of the Concord and crossing the bridge on foot in this violent weather.

Kicking off his brake, Bledsoe put his leaders and swing-spanners on the bridge decking. The horses protested, then lunged forward reluctantly under Bledsoe's whip, the howling gale thinning off his vitrolic profanity.

Midway across the puncheon span, a flash of lightning overhead revealed a great cottonwood tree sweeping down the river toward the bridge, its gnarled roots forming a battering ram which might easily rip the trestlework out from under the span.

With a hoarse bawl of terror, Bledsoe stood up in the driver's seat and tried to lash his team into a run as the lightning flash was followed by Stygian blackness.

Then the driving drift log struck the central pier of the trestle with a splintering crash which carried to Bledsoe's ears above the cacophony of the tempest.

The planks ahead buckled downward like a V, the six-horse team falling through the gape in the bridge. Bledsoe felt the Concord up-end under him, and he was hurled out into space, still clinging to his leather ribbons.

Inside the coach, Ranger Jim Hatfield felt the girl thrown violently against him as the Concord plummeted down into the raging waters, momentarily held motionless by a tangle of bridge timbers and driftwood.

With only seconds in which to work, Hatfield clawed a key from the hatband of his Stetson and, as Les Radley was thrown against him by the slow capsizing of the stagecoach, he managed to unlock the iron bracelet which girdled the outlaw's wrist. Fettered together, they would both drown. Singly, they had a fighting chance.

The Colorado drummer's scream was like that of a woman as the two-hundred-pound man found himself jammed on top of the cursing Radley. Then the stage seemed to crack apart as the howling river tore the running gear and the harnessed team free of the coach.

In the darkness, Hatfield tried to grip the girl's arm as he felt himself hurled out through the hole ripped in the roof of the Concord. Then he felt his hand torn from the girl's sleeve and he was under water, caught in the irresistible grip of the churning current.

Dimly, as he came to the surface, Hatfield glimpsed the broken skeleton of the bridge. Somewhere off to his left the stage team, tangled in the harness, was being swept down the canyon. He heard the drummer's gargling scream, heard it cut off as the fat man went under.

The savage force of the current swept the Ranger against the west bank and he clawed for a hold on the dwarf willows which grew above the crest of the flood. Pure luck had thrown him into shallow water. But, hampered by his oilskin slicker, he knew that swimming would have been little short of impossible.

Pulling himself to a ledge of rock, the Lone Wolf jerked off the torn remnants of his slicker and hurled them aside. The rain had ceased and breaks appeared in the scudding slate-gray clouds overhead, where the argent glow of a full moon sent spotlight beams penciling down on the ruined bridge and the span of river leading up to the rock where Hatfield had gained refuge.

He climbed to the canyon rim twenty feet above, probing the river's surface for a glimpse of the other three passengers and the old jehu. A blur of movement far downstream caused the Ranger to swing his gaze to the southward. He was in time to see a drenched figure in an oilskin slicker climbing off a drifting log to the safety of an outjutting claybank.

"Radley made it—"

Hatfield ground out the words as he reached for the

guns which rode the waterlogged holsters at his thighs. Radley, half-drowned, was a good hundred yards down canyon. Hatfield's duty as a Ranger was clear.

He headed toward the smuggler, who was crawling like a wounded snake out on the cactus-tufted rim of the canyon, limned vividly against a patch of moonlit sky. And then, dimly to Hatfield's ears above the churning of angry waters below him, he heard a woman's scream.

Wheeling, the Ranger peered down to catch sight of the girl passenger, clinging to a red-and-yellow door which the flood had jerked off the Concord. The door had jammed between two rocks, out in midriver. At any moment the water, spuming over the rocks, would jerk the door clear and doom the girl.

Hatfield's hopes to capture his escaped prisoner were dashed, in the face of this new emergency. He unbuckled the burden of his double-shell belts, kicked off his star red boots, and removed his bullhide chaps, knowing that they would make swimming difficult.

Then, heading for a spot on the rimrock twenty yards upstream from where the girl clung to her uncertain support, Jim Hatfield flung off the Stetson which his chin-cord had held in place and, palms together, did a swan dive out into space.

He hit the river in a geyser of spray and went under. When he surfaced, the racing current had carried him almost on top of the jutting boulders where the girl clung.

Swimming with hard strokes, Hatfield fought his way out of the side currents which formed a fork on either side of the rocks, and a moment later was flung violently against Beth Beloud. The shock of their impact dislodged the stage door from the rocks, then they were both in swimming water, unable to cling to the boulder.

The current flung them past the claybank where Les Radley had crawled to safety, and they were being borne down a series of rapids between looming rock walls.

With one hand clinging to the girl's hair, Hatfield fought to get clear of the current, his legs hammering over submerged rocks, the girl's body a dead weight which impeded his efforts.

Moonlight glinted on a rising fog of spray which told of a waterfall dead ahead. Taxing his muscles to the utmost, the Lone Wolf cranked an elbow around the girl's head and, taking advantage of a whirlpool, managed to grab the overhanging limb of a riverband cottonwood, its trunk half submerbed by the flood.

The cottonwood limb cracked under their weight, and Hatfield groaned as he felt the limb arc around. If it broke, they would be thrown on the very lip of the waterfall, to certain death on the talus rocks where the Tornillo's flood was pounding.

But the limb held, long enough for Hatfield to feel solid rock beneath his sock-clad feet. Hugging the girl's limp body to him with his left arm, the Ranger braced himself against the water's rush and, running the gamble for what it was worth, let go the fractured tree limb.

The cottonwood branch whipped around and broke off, to vanish over the crest of the waterfall. But Jim Hatfield, jackknifing the girl's insensible form over his shoulder, waded out of hip-deep water to gain the safety of a sloping ledge free of the river's surging tentacles.

He carried his burden up to the rimrock and lowered her to the ground, sinking beside her. His strength was spent. For the first time he became aware of his own wracking coughs, as he dispelled muddy river water from his lungs.

Lying there, momentarily helpless, Hatfield thought of Les Radley, and shrugged. The smuggler could make his escape now, and the Lone Wolf would have a failure to report to Roaring Bill McDowell. But at the moment, this break of bad luck seemed unimportant, compared to the human life he had saved.

He saw a rolling object go over the waterfall's crest and vanish in the moonlit spray fifty feet below. That would be the drowned corpse of the drummer. Down in the rapids below the waterfall, he made out the carcasses of the stage team, with the front wheels of the stage still hooked to the harness, like the remains of a Roman chariot. The rest of the ill-fated Wells Fargo coach would be scattered like kindling wood for miles down the Tornillo, eventually to float into the mighty Rio Grande.

CHAPTER III

Stolen Guns

Looming against the skyline above the canyon brink, Hatfield saw the peaked outlines of a deserted cabin, and was reminded that this had once been a way station on the stagecoach line, before Comanches had massacred the stock tender and his family.

The shack offered shelter against the frigid wind which howled down off the Big Bend peaks on the trail of the rainstorm, and Hatfield knew that continued exposure to this cold could mean pneumonia for the girl he had rescued. Lifting her in his arms, the Ranger scrambled up the slope and entered the cabin. Its roof was gone, burned out by the Indian raiders of long ago, but the sturdy rock and adobe walls cut off the windy blasts.

He laid the girl down on an ancient bunk in one corner and felt for her pulse. It was strong and rapid. She was breathing easily, which was proof that she had not taken in much water. Then he saw a bloody welt on her temple, and realized that she had been knocked out when the river had torn them between the twin rocks out in the canyon.

Convinced that she would rally out of her torpor in due time, Hatfield scraped up dry leaves and trash from the cabin floor and, thanks to a waterproof match box formed of two .45-70 cartridges fitted end to end, got a fire going in the fireplace. He broke up a split-pole chair and table to furnish substantial fuel for the fire. Then, after another glance at the girl, he made his way outside.

He followed the river bank ledge upstream until he came to the spot where he had seen Les Radley. He was not surprised to see that the smuggler had long since vanished. Boot prints in the mud revealed where Radley had crossed the stagecoach road and headed into the chaparral beyond.

The handcuffs still dangled from Hatfield's left wrist, but somewhere along the line he had lost the key. He headed on up the rimrock, found his Stetson and chaps and donned them.

A little further on he located his boots and thrust his bleeding feet into them. It was not until he stood up that he saw that his shell belts and holstered Colts were missing.

"Radley doubled back up the road and spotted my artillery," the Ranger groaned. "That makes me a prime target for an ambush."

Hatfield faded back into the brush, shivering in the cold. The odds were all in Radley's favor now. If the smuggler knew that his erstwhile captor had escaped the flood, Radley's presence in this vicinity would be a constant threat to Hatfield's safety.

A short distance through the brush, the Ranger came to a game trail which snaked off into the Rosillos uplands in the direction of Thundergust Basin, beyond the divide. Radley's tracks were plain to read in this trail. The outlaw had not tarried long at the scene of disaster.

Ordinarily, Hatfield would have set out in immediate pursuit of his quarry, knowing that he had a fair chance of overtaking the fugitive. If Radley stopped to rest, there was always the chance that Hatfield could attack him from ambush and nullify the fact that Radley had stolen his guns.

But now he had the girl to think about. He could not leave her at the deserted shack until he was positive she had not been seriously injured by her ordeal in the river.

Reluctantly, Hatfield turned away from Radley's trail and returned to the riverbank cabin. Smoke was spiraling from the chimney of the roofless shack. The interior was a ruddy glow from the fireplace blaze.

Even as he stepped into the one-room cabin, Hatfield saw that his worries were over. The girl had left the bunk and stood with her back to the fireplace, steam wisping from her sopped skirt and bodice. Even with her hair plastered tight to her skull, and her face bloodied from the wound on her temple, he saw that she was uncommonly beautiful.

"I—I owe you my life, Mr. Radley!" the girl said huskily, staring across the cabin at the man in the doorway. "Whatever the law may think of you, I shall never forget that."

Hatfield's grin faded from his lips. For some reason, this victim of the bridge accident believe he was an outlaw!

"My name is Beth Beloud," the girl went on, before Hatfield could correct her mistake. "I was heading for Alto. My father owned the Rafter B ranch over in Thundergust Basin. I've fallen heir to it. But if it hadn't been for you, Mr. Radley, I should never have lived to claim my legacy."

Hatfield stepped into the glow of the fireplace, squatting there to let the welcome heat soak into his aching flesh. The shuttering firelight revealed him as a black-haired, black-browed man, ruggedly handsome, in spite of his gauntness and his unshaven jaws. His eyes were what struck the girl as the most unusual and at the same time, his most attractive feature. They were of a peculiar greenish shade, the hue of an iceberg's edge when salt waters washed it.

Hatfield came to his feet, looking down at the girl. Under the pressure of more urgent thoughts, he had already forgotten the fact that she believed him to be Les Radley. Under different circumstances, her mistake would have amused him. But now his prime purpose was to get on the smuggler's trail without delay, perilous though such a pursuit would be.

"When daylight comes, ma'am," he said in a deep-chested bass, "yuh'll find a trail down the road about fifty yards. That trail will lead yuh to Alto, just over the divide. It's not over fifteen miles from here. I—I'm afraid I'll have to leave yuh, now that I know yuh're unharmed. Yuh see, the man I was handcuffed to is a man I—"

Beth Beloud's soft laugh cut him off as she touched his wet sleeve with a hand which wore, he noticed, a diamond solitaire. She was engaged to marry some lucky man, then.

"I understand perfectly, Mr. Radley," she said, glancing at the steel manacles which dangled from his left wrist. "Wait! Perhaps you can use this to get rid of that bracelet."

As she spoke, Beth opened a velvet reticule which had been looped about her wrist and which, miraculously, she had not lost following the stagecoach's plunge from the broken bridge. From the reticule the girl drew out a small pearl-handled .32 pistol.

Hatfield grinned as he accepted the gun. Holding the muzzle against the handcuff lock, he pulled trigger. The water-proof shell exploded, and the fetters dropped from Hatfield's wrist as the bullet sprung the lock.

"*Muchas gracias,* Miss Beloud." The Ranger grinned. "Now, about me being named Radley—"

He was in the act of informing her that he was a Texas Ranger, not an outlaw; but a vagrant thought crossed the edge of his mind then, and he did not finish the sentence. The town of Alto was the nearest settlement, and Hatfield knew Alto to be a notorious outlaw nest, here on the rugged Rosillos.

Les Radley would, in all probability, head for Alto tonight, for the town was a way point on the notorious Tombstone Trail, and Radley no doubt had friends there who would shelter him. This girl was heading for Alto in the morning, and Jim Hatfield had reasons of his own for not wanting his identity to be known in that lawless town.

"I'll keep your secret, Mr. Radley," Beth Beloud told

him. "You—you keep that pistol. I at least owe you that much."

He shook his head, thrusting the little gun back into her reticule.

"No thanks, ma'am," he said drily. "I think yuh'll be safe hoofin' it over to Thundergust Basin, but this is wild country and I'd rather yuh had some protection."

Hatfield removed his Stetson and ran strong bronzed fingers through his wet hair. He was dog-tired, and nothing would have pleased him more than to have remained before this crackling fire, shielded from the night's icy winds.

But one of Texas' most-wanted owlhooters had slipped out of his clutches tonight, and every moment he delayed here cut down his chances of overtaking Les Radley.

Crossing the room, Hatfield paused on the threshold of the cabin door and she caught the full strike of the fire's glow on his even white teeth as he smiled in farewell.

"*Hasta la vista*, ma'am," the Ranger said, and then he was gone.

For a long moment, Beth Beloud stood staring at the empty doorway, mingled emotions surging through her.

She was a product of a Big Bend cattle ranch, was Beth Beloud, and as such she was no stranger to the perils of the frontier. Her mother had been killed and scalped by Indians when she was an infant. She had seen men die with gunsmoke in their nostrils as a result of range wars, during her adolescent years. With her own hands she had bandaged wounded men, some of them outlaws, who had come to her father's Rafter B for refuge.

Yet in all her twenty-one years Beth had never met a man on the dodge who affected her as strangely as had this ruggedly built young Texan whom she believed to be the kingpin outlaw of them all, Les Radley.

His smile, the frankness of his eyes, the risk he had run in saving her from certain doom in the Tornillo's raging flood tonight—these things, great and small, were factors which she found difficult to ascribe to a man who had such a craven and bestial reputation as Les Radley had. The courtesy and bravery of this man she had encountered tonight had been matched by only one other man she had known in her life—old Captain Bob Beloud, her martyred father.

Thoughts of the old captain, one of Jeb Stuart's heroes before he had returned from the wars and had met and married Beth's mother, brought tears to the girl's eyes as she crouched beside the fireplace, absorbing its warmth.

From her plush reticule she drew out an envelope addressed to her at the college she had been attending in Austin. The envelope contained two letters, which were wet and limp now, the inked text blurred and thinned by immersion in the river.

She spread the soggy paper out on the hearthstone to dry, rereading the messages which had brought such a change in her life. The first was from Leon Hesterling, foreman of the Rafter B, the man to whom Beth was engaged and planned to marry as soon as she finished her senior year at college. It read:

Beth Darling:

Since telegraphing you that your father was mysteriously killed from ambush, I have become more than ever convinced that he was a victim of Tombstone Trail smugglers who use Rafter B range in crossing to and from Mexico.

I cannot urge you too emphatically to leave school and return to Thundergust Basin, even though we could not delay your father's funeral long enough for you to attend it. As foreman of the Rafter B, I strongly advise you to sell this ranch for what it will bring. We can be married and start our lives together somewhere away from the Tombstone Trail. Please telegraph me in care of the Blue Casino in Alto that you are either coming home, or that you grant me power of attorney so that I can sell the Rafter B.

The other letter, written only two weeks ago, was from her late father's cavvy wrangler, Dall Stockton, an orphan kid who had been adopted by Captain Beloud and who, growing up with Beth, had always cherished her like a sister. It was Stockton's letter which had made the girl decide to leave school and pay the Rafter B a visit, rather than telegraphing her fiancé permission to sell the small-tally spread where she had been born and raised.

Dall's letter read:

Dear Beth—

Maybe I am sticking my horns into something that ain't any of my business, but I wouldn't let Leon Hesterling rush you into selling out the Rafter B. Grote Postell, who owns the Coffin 13 outfit and who is out to hog all the range in the Basin, has offered to buy your dad's ranch, but in spite of what your future husband says about smugglers killing the Captain, I think that Postell's Coffin 13 riders bushwhacked your father, Beth. Whatever you decide to do, you know you can count on me to back you to the last turn of the cards.

Like Always,

Dall

When the two letters were thoroughly dried, Beth returned them to her reticule. Whether her father had been killed by Tombstone Trail *contrabandistas*, or had been dropped by a bullet from a rival cattle outfit, Beth knew that she had inherited plenty of trouble when the Rafter B had passed into her hands. At the moment, she was not sure whether she wanted to follow her fiancé's advice and sell the home ranch, or whether, as Dall Stockton had hinted, she should remain in Thundergust Basin and fight the powerful Coffin 13 spread which dominated the Basin's grazing range.

Here in this wind-lashed, roofless cabin within earshot of the angry waters of Tornillo Creek, it was difficult for Beth to realize that she had brushed eternity so close tonight. Now that her benefactor was gone, tonight's events seemed more than ever like a nightmare, something that had never happened.

CHAPTER IV

Owlhoot Town

Dawn found Jim Hatfield plodding doggedly along the Indian trace which led over the backbone of the Rosillos. He had tarried in the vicinity of the washed-out bridge only long enough to locate the drowned body of old Zeke Bedloe, the driver. The veteran Wells-Fargo reinsman had died of a crushed skull when he had been hurled from the Concord, his body trapped in the splintered timbers below the bridge, half-submerged by the rushing waters.

With the fourth and last human soul accounted for after tonight's tragedy, the Lone Wolf Ranger set out on Radley's trail. He was certain that the Tombstone Trail outlaw had struck out for Alto town, across the summit, in the belief that his erstwhile captor had been swept to his death over the Tornillo waterfall.

Nevertheless, Hatfield followed the trail with the utmost caution, knowing that he would be a target for an ambush if Radley stopped to rest and discovered that he was being trailed.

Shortly before sunrise, the tag-end of the rainstorm wheeled back across the Rosillos and the resulting downpour turned the Indian trail into a river of mud, thoroughly obliterating the boot prints which Hatfield was following. By daybreak the storm had blown itself out and the Texas sky was like blue enamel, warm and benevolent after the two-day storm.

Topping the Rosillos divide, Hatfield had a breath-taking vista of the vast mountain-girdled reach of Thundergust Basin. Ten miles across, the Basin was hemmed in by the Rosillos on the east and by the loftier, granite-toothed and arroyo-gashed range of the Corazones on the west. The two mountain systems met to the north, forming that boundary of the basin. Twenty miles to the south loomed the great, shadowy gorge of the Rio Grande, with Chihuahua's bleak uplands lifting in purple corrugations beyond.

From this lofty elevation, the green grama flats of the basin were mottled with darker splotches which the Ranger knew were cattle. Down in the Rosillos spurs below him, he saw the toylike barns and corrals and outbuildings of a big cattle outfit, which, from his advance knowledge of the region, he guessed would be Grote Postell's powerful Coffin 13 headquarters.

Another ranch, a mere blur in the distance, lay between creases of the Corazones foothills to the westward. Off-hand, Jim Hatfield tabbed that outfit as the Rafter B, which belonged to Beth Beloud, the girl he had rescued.

Nearer at hand, toward the south, and hidden from view by an intervening ridge, Hatfield saw plumes of smoke lifting against the purple vista of the Mexican badlands. That would mark the location of Alto, the first Texas settlement on the old Spanish route now known as the Tombstone Trail and, in all likelihood Les Radley's destination.

With his head start, the escaped smuggler probably was already at the town. Hatfield headed on down the muddy trail in that direction, wrestling with the problem that would face him when he arrived in the outlaw settlement.

His duties as a Ranger had never brought him to Alto before, so he knew he was reasonably safe from being spotted as a Ranger. But, without weapons, he would be taking his life in his hands the moment he arrived at the town. Les Radley would not hesitate to gun him down on sight.

A mile further down the trail, Hatfield came to a triple fork, like the prongs of a trident. The right-hand trail snaked off down the foot slopes in the direction of the Coffin 13 Ranch; the main trail pointed toward Alto. The left-hand fork followed the ridge of the mountain range, toward Mexico and the Tombstone Trail ford of the Rio Grande.

In the act of heading on down the Alto trail, a glint of morning sun rays on metal drew Hatfield's alert eye toward the left-hand trail. Acting on a hunch, he headed toward the flash of light, which came from a clump of ocotillo cactus several yards off the trail and down the wall of a ravine.

Without leaving the trail, Hatfield identified the metal which had reflected the sunlight. It was the hasp of a badly-torn oilskin slicker, which he recognized instantly as the one Les Radley had worn en route from Paisano Pass to the stagecoach depot on the Tornillo flats.

"Which means Radley must be headin' directly to Mexico," Hatfield pondered. "And too much of a head start for me to catch up with him this side of the Rio Grande."

He followed the ridge line trail for a mile, on the off-chance that he might come upon Radley at a camp and capture him while he slept. Numerous side trails intersected this route, all of them converging on the canyon in which Alto was located.

Radley might have veered off the Mexican trail by any one of these side paths. After all, this was Radley's home territory. He might have chosen this method of reaching Alto instead of following along the direct trail.

Emerging from dense mesquite and cat-claw thickets, Hatfield caught sight of the tar-paper roofs and false-fronted buildings of Alto, a mile down the canyon. Hunger was consuming the Ranger and he was well aware of the fact that trailing Radley, from here on, would be the blindest kind of guesswork.

Accordingly, the Lone Wolf took the next trail leading to Alto and, an hour later, found himself on the outskirts of the mountain town which overlooked the Thundergust Basin rangeland. The stagecoach road across the mountains formed a muddy ribbon which connected with Alto's main street. This, in reality, was the outlaw avenue of the Tombstone Trail.

Entering the town cautiously from the uphill slope, Hatfield found a Chinese restaurant on a side street and, going inside, ordered the first square meal he had eaten in two weeks.

With his appetite satisfied, Hatfield found his spirits in much better shape. His first objective now was obvious —he needed a six-gun and ammunition.

Emerging onto the main street, the Ranger sized up the thoroughfare cautiously before leaving the alley between the two saloons which had brought him over from the Chinese restaurant. At this early hour, most of the deadfalls and honkatonks were closed. A few Coffin 13 cow ponies lined the hitchracks in front of a false-fronted gambling hall labeled the "Blue Casino." Hatfield noted that the proprietor's name was Grote Postell. He was the owner of the biggest ranch in the basin, the Coffin 13.

A few yards down the street, Hatfield saw a small adobe shack which was identified by a ten-foot wooden six-shooter as a gunsmith's shop. He paid a visit to this establishment and, after considerable haggling with the bald-headed proprietor, used the last of his available cash to purchase a rusty Colt .45 Peacemaker, a shabby holster and a shell-belt.

The gunsmith, sizing up his customer as a man on the dodge, condescended to throw in a handful of .45 cartridges free.

After hefting the gun and getting the feel of its hammer and trigger mechanism, Jim Hatfield left the shop and headed in the direction of the Overland Telegraph office. His saddle horse, Goldy, was stabled at Ranger district headquarters in Presidio, and Hatfield felt like a fish out of water without a mount.

A discreetly worded telegram to the Presidio Rangers would result in Goldy's being dispatched here to Alto. In addition, Hatfield knew that he had to notify his superior, Roaring Bill McDowell, of what had happened to Les Radley.

En route to the telegraph office, Hatfield passed the wide-open archway of a livery barn from which issued the pleasant odors of hay and horseflesh and oiled leather. A big sign painted on the warped gable of the stable identified it as the "Tombstone Trail Livery, Saml Rome, Prop."

While passing the stable office, a placard on the door caught Hatfield's eye. It read:

HOSTLER WANTED, $10 A WEEK.
APPLY WITHIN. NIGHT SHIFT.

The Ranger hesitated. He had already made up his mind to stick around Alto a few days, in the hope that Les Radley would show up. To do so, however, would invite the curiosity of the outlaw town unless he had some tangible excuse for being here.

Spurred by a hunch, Hatfield stepped into the Tombstone Trail Livery office and confronted the rawboned, overall-clad oldster who was busily engaged in soaping a saddle.

"I'll take that hostler's job, if it's still open," Hatfield said, grinning. "You Mr. Rome?"

The oldster nodded, sizing up his applicant's rangy six-foot figure, noting his unshaven condition, his muddy chaps and boots, the rust on his single Colt.

"I'm Rome," the stableman grunted, spitting a gobbet of tobacco juice at a knothole in the floor and missing it by a wide margin. "Had experience groomin' hosses? Know how to mend wagons? Know how to treat bobwire cuts and gall sores?"

Jim Hatfield shrugged, reaching in his shirt pocket for makings, and discovering that his tobacco and thin husks had been ruined by river water.

"I ain't a licensed vet, if that's what you're expectin' to hire for ten pesos a week," he countered. "But I been a brushpoppin' cowhand all my life."

Rome scratched his jaw thoughtfully.

"Where's yore hoss, son?"

Hatfield shook his head. "Hoofed it here."

Rome grunted knowingly. "Either sold yore saddle or yuh're on the dodge. Yore kind usually wind up in Alto. Law sniffin' yore back tracks?"

Hatfield turned as if to leave.

"If yuh ain't satisfied with my pedigree and earmarks," he drawled. "I ain't yore man."

Sam Rome gestured hastily with his awl.

"Hold on, feller. The job's yore's. Only, if yuh're on the dodge, I want to warn yuh about Vic Drumm. He's the sheriff hereabouts. A bounty-hunter who'd sell yuh down the river for a five-dollar reward . . . What's your name?"

"Yuh can call me Field," the Ranger said. "James J. Field."

Rome reached in his pocket and fished out a roll of bills. He handed Hatfield a ten-dollar banknote.

"Week's pay in advance," Rome grunted. "I'll take my chances on yuh driftin' through. Yuh'll work the night shift, dark to daylight. Down the street yonder is the only hotel in town, the Alto House. Tell the clerk I sent yuh down and he'll fix yuh up with a room at four bits a night. Report back here at sundown."

Hatfield grinned his thanks and stepped out into the sunlight. He was quartering across the wheel-rutted street, planning to visit the Overland Telegraph office before engaging his room at the Alto House, when he was startled to hear someone call him by name from the porch of the Blue Casino gambling dive.

Hand plummeting instinctively to gunbutt, the Ranger whirled, to stare in the direction of the voice. It seemed impossible that he had been recognized, within an hour after reaching Alto.

Then he saw a tall, dusky-skinned Mexican girl stepping out across the plank sidewalk toward him. She was wearing a gaudy red-and-yellow fandango costume, her arms bangled with cheap jewelry, an artifical rose pinned in her raven-black tresses.

"Don't you remember Zolanda, Senor Jeem?" the girl bantered, cocking her head at an angle and regarding him coquettishly.

Hatfield stared, recognition stirring him. This was a dancehall girl he had known years ago in Del Rio, at the start of his Ranger career. Zolanda Ruiz, her name was. But more startling still, Hatfield knew her as Les Radley's wife!

CHAPTER V

Zolanda's Story

Hatfield glanced quickly up and down the street, and was relieved to see that no one was within earshot. As long as he remained in Alto, his own safety depended upon being incognito. Knowing the reputation of this Big Bend cowtown, he knew that a Texas Ranger would be fair game for perhaps two-thirds of the population here.

Zolanda Ruiz' appearance from out of the past could be both a blessing and a threat to Hatfield's plans. The girl's very presence in Alto pointed to the fact that Les Radley might be making his home here. On the other hand, Zolanda knew that Hatfield was a Ranger, and would tip off Radley that a lawman had come to Alto under an assumed name.

"Howdy, Zolanda," the Lone Wolf greeted her, reaching out to shake her beringed hand. "Long time no see. Yuh was packin' the cowboys into the Del Rio fandango parlors the last time our trails crossed. Yuh're as lovely as ever."

Hatfield's compliment was stretching the truth a bit on the side of gallantry, and the *bailerina* sensed as much for her black eyes clouded wistfully. When the Ranger had first known Zolanda, she had been sixteen, just flowering into womanhood, and her dance routines had been pure fluid poetry in their perfection.

But the years had not been kind to Zolanda. Her hair, once the ebon sheen of a *zopilote's* plumage, was streaked with gray threads now, which she had tried unsuccessfully to dye. Her corseted body was on the fleshy side, as was the case with many Mexican women when they reached their late thirties, and her once-haunting eyes had lost their lustre and were brooding and tragic behind artificial lashes.

"You are steel the gallant *embustero*, how you say ze liar in Engleesh," she chided him, flirting a Spanish fan. "Eet grieves me to know that once when I was young and beautiful, I was een love weeth you, Senor Jeem. But you had no eyes for leetle Zolanda. I theenk a leetle corner of my heart has always been yours, *amigo.*"

Hatfield flushed with embarrassment.

"A man in my—er—job hasn't time for love," he answered somberly. "No woman wants a man when she knows she might become a widow at any time."

Zolanda discarded her bantering manner, peering up into the Ranger's eyes with blinkless intensity. He was not wearing his law badge, preferring to work alone and under cover, a habit which had given him his nickname of the "Lone Wolf."

"You are steel a *Rangero, no es verdad?*" the girl asked bluntly, lowering her voice.

Hatfield hesitated. It was entirely possible that this woman had been in Les Radley's arms this very morning. Perhaps the outlaw was asleep at this moment in Zolanda's home here in Alto, resting up after his recent ordeal.

"We got a lot of old times to discuss, *querida mia,*" he said, with an impersonal smile. "Yuh live here in Alto? Mebbe we could find a quiet place to visit a while."

If she divined that he was trying to entice her into leading him to her husband's hideout, she gave no sign of such suspicion. She gestured toward Grote Postell's gambling house with her fan.

"I am dancing at the Blue Casino for my leeving, Senor Jeem," she said. "I leeve upstairs over the barroom, *si.* But my dressing *sala* ees downstairs. We talk there, no?"

Loosening his gun in holster, Hatfield accompanied the gaily dressed dancehall girl down an alley alongside the Blue Casino, saw her mount a short flight of steps which led to her dressing room doorway. Every nerve and sinew in the Ranger's body was taut as he kept close behind Zolanda Ruiz, knowing that Les Radley might be waiting behind cocked guns on the other side of that door.

But the girl entered the little room without hesitating, and as Hatfield crossed the threshold, he saw that he was safe here. The little *sala* had no curtained-off closets where Radley might be hiding. The door opened against a wall.

Zolanda seated herself at a three-mirrored dressing table and waved Hatfield to a sofa opposite her as he closed the alley door and finished his quick appraisal of the room. The air was cloying, from cheap perfume and theatrical make-up. The walls were hung with garish-hued dancing costumes, serapes, and big Mexican hats which Zolanda used in her dance numbers.

"You are steel a *Rangero?*" She repeated the question he had evaded answering out on the street.

As she spoke she offered him a packet of black Mexican *cigarillos*, but he declined the smoke. He was extremely wary of treachery, and knew that a cigarette could contain deadly opiates.

Zolanda shrugged, removed a cigarette from the pack and stuck it between her painted lips. Hatfield took the last dry match from his cartridge-case container and lighted it for her, abashed at his own suspicious attitude.

"Yes, Zolanda," he said frankly. "I'm still a Ranger."

Through clouding smoke, the Mexican girl eyed him fondly.

"But *es seguro*. The most famous *Rangero* een Texas. *El Lobo Solo*, the Lone Wolf . . . What breengs you to Alto pueblo, Jeem?"

Again Hatfield heard a warning tocsin in the back of his head. Was Zolanda feeling him out, fishing for information which she would relay to her outlaw husband, hiding perhaps in her upstairs bedroom over the Blue Casino?

"Just passing through, *amiga mia.*" He paused, eyeing her sharply. "How goes married life, Zolanda? Is Les Radley good to you?"

Zolanda's black eyes flashed wickedly as she pursed her lips and blew a chain of delicate smoke rings toward Hatfield.

"Bah!" she spat out angrily. "Do not mention that name to me, Senor Jeem. I weesh never to see that *ladrone* again."

The Ranger leaned forward, his interest quickening. "You are no longer married to Radley?"

She shrugged her shoulders. "*Si.* My religious faith does not permit what thos' gringo women call the divorce, Jeem. But I have not leev' weeth Les Radley for ten year now. Else why am I dancing een a honkytonk like thees one, eh?"

Hatfield rubbed his stubbled jaw thoughtfully. If Zolanda was telling him the truth, perhaps he had found a valuable ally rather than a potential traitor to his cause. And, with his keen judgment for sizing up human nature, he believed Zolanda was being frank with him in regard to her husband.

"What happened to yore marriage?" he asked casually. "Shorely Les knew he had a prize when he married yuh back in Del Rio."

Zolanda Ruiz drew on her black cigarette for a moment before answering.

"Radley ees not a man to be faithful to one woman," she said. "He discarded me like the cast-off shirt when my beauty began to fade. I hate heem, Senor Jeem. I would gladly steek a *cuchillo* een hees black heart, that ees so."

She spoke with a violent Latin intensity which—unless she were a consummate actress—could not be mistaken. To girls like Zolanda Ruiz, hate and love were passions of equal intensity.

"I'm sorry to hear it," Hatfield temporized. "Radley will never meet a finer girl than you, Zolanda. I mean that sincerely."

Tears misted in the dancer's eyes as she leaned forward, regarding him with tender benevolence.

"Senor Jeem, let me warn you. Thees town ees not for a *Rangero* to find himself een. The sheriff, Senor Vic Drumm, ees a *malo hombre*. The man who owns thees Casino, Senor Postell—he ees a *maldito vaquero*. There are a hundred hombres een Alto thees very day who would shoot you een the back eef they knew you were a *Ranger Tejano*. You must not stay here, Jeem."

Hatfield smiled tolerantly.

"I've got a job as a hostler over at Sam Rome's stable, Zolanda. No man will know I am a Ranger—if you keep yore mouth shut. Are yuh my friend? Can I count on yore loyalty?"

The woman flicked her cigarette aside and smiled gently.

"Fire could not torture your secret from me, Jeem," she said passionately. "You get work at Senor Rome's leevery barn? Then that means you come to Alto as a man-hunter. What *ladrone* are you seeking een these pueblo, Jeem?"

Again the Lone Wolf found himself reluctant to commit himself, half-doubting Zolanda's sincerity, yet remembering that as a girl she had had a romantic affection for him, a love which he had not reciprocated. That alone, he realized, might make Zolanda hate him, masking that hate behind a front of friendship.

"Alto is a well-known outlaw den," he countered. "Tombstone Trail smugglers hide out in this town. I should not have to look far to find fair game, Zolanda."

For a long moment, she was silent. A pulse throbbed at the V of her neck and she fisted and unfisted her hands on her lap, as if struggling with an inward decision.

"Senor Jeem," she whispered finally, "what would you geeve to know where Les Radley ees hiding?"

Hatfield masked his sharpened interest behind a shrug.

"Radley is wanted by the Rangers for killin'," he said. "If I knew where Radley was hidin', my duty would be to send him to the gallows, Zolanda."

Zolanda got to her feet and paced a circuit around the room. Finally she whirled with a swish of silken skirts and, hands akimbo on hips, stared down at the Ranger.

"I owe Radley no wifely loyalty," she said in Spanish. "He broke our marriage vows." Lowering her voice to a whisper, Zolanda said: "Radley is hiding on a *pastor's* sheep ranch out in Paisano Pass, Jeem. That I know for a certainty."

Hatfield saw her relax, spent and gasping by the emotional strain she had been under in bracing herself to voice this betrayal of the *esposo* who had discarded her in favor of younger women.

Hatfield knew the truth now, knew he could trust this woman. And, relying on that conviction, he told her in terse phrases the story of Radley's capture and subsequent escape, and the reason for his own presence here in Alto.

"If Radley hasn't headed for Mexico, I figger he'll turn up here in Alto sooner or later," the Lone Wolf concluded. "That's why I'm posin' as one of Sam Rome's stable hands while I'm in town, Zolanda."

A knock on the inner door of the dressing room startled the couple. A gruff voice issued from the barroom:

"Yore act is on in twenty minutes, Zolanda. The Red Duke has offered to pay the house fifty dollars in gold if yuh do yore sombrero number. Make shore yuh do it, understand?"

Zolanda called back her assent, and then turned to Hatfield.

"That was Grote Postell," she whispered. "You weel be out front to see my act, Jeem? Remember how I used to do the 'Hat Dance' for you back in Del Rio—before I married Les Radley and unhappiness came to ruin my life?"

Jim Hatfield grinned, getting to his feet.

"I'll see yore act," he promised her. "Remember, Zolanda—my safety is in yore hands. I know yuh won't double-cross me."

CHAPTER VI

Dead Man's Poker Hand

On leaving Zolanda Ruiz' dressing room, Hatfield made a circuit of the Blue Casino outside, and entered the gambling hall from the street entrance. Although it was mid-afternoon, the place was crowded with gun-hung, spurred and booted customers.

Standing unobtrusively along the wall by the batwings, Jim Hatfield sized up the establishment and came to the mental conclusion that if Alto was a sinkhole of outlawry, Grote Postell's palace of chance was the pit and core of the town's wickedness. Most of the customers lining the bar had the ferret-eyed look of men on the dodge, rustlers and *contrabandistas* from both sides of the Rio Grande.

A roulette table had attracted most of the cowpunchers whom Hatfield judged were from the Coffin 13 outfit. Most of the poker tables in the hall were going full blast.

At the far end of the barroom was an elevated stage, in front of which a Negro pianist was jangling out ragtime tunes. The stage curtains were drawn, their tasseled bottoms lit up by a row of shielded kerosene footlights. That proscenium, then, was where Zolanda Ruiz would make her appearance shortly, to entertain Postell's customers.

Hatfield made his way to the bar, bought a sack of Durham and a book of wheat-straw cigarette papers, then located a vacant chair in one corner of the Casino, given over to a billiard table. While he was rolling a cigarette, a man dropped into the barrel chair beside him and Hatfield recognized his livery stable boss, Sam Rome.

"Sizin' up the town before yuh go to work in it, Field?" Rome chuckled. "Well, yuh come to the right spot. That's Grote Postell over by the chuckaluck cage.

Get this straight—Postell not only runs the Blue Casino, but he runs Alto and the sheriff and his Coffin Thirteen spread takes in most of Thundergust Basin."

Cementing his quirly with a swipe of his tongue, Hatfield glanced in the direction of Rome's indicating finger. Grote Postell was a towerng figure in a black fustian town coat and green Keevil hat. He easily dominated the crowd.

Postell's florid-face was set off by bushy black brows which covered his deep-set eyes like awnings. The predatory line of his mouth was accentuated by a close-clipped black mustache, and he had a ten-inch Cuban perfecto gripped between gold-capped teeth. A nugget chain was looped across his flowered vest. His Hussar-style boots were polished to a high gloss, and the sunflower rowels of his Mexican spurs were plated with gleaming yellow gold.

Everything about the gun-boss of Alto seemed to advertise the man's ruthless arrogance. A range baron, Hatfield already knew that Postell ruled the Thundergust Basin cattle business. From what Rome hinted, the local bounty-hunting sheriff, Vic Drumm, wore Postell's collar also.

Hatfield's glance slid off the Blue Casino boss and searched the smoke-clouded barroom, on the off-chance that Les Radley might be rubbing shoulders with the Border riffraff congregated here. His attention was distracted by Sam Rome's plucking his shirt sleeve.

"Another hombre yuh ought to know is the Coffin Thirteen foreman, Jepp Vozar," the liveryman whispered, jerking his thumb toward a waddy who was playing stud poker at a nearby table. "Vozar is Postell's right-hand man. He runs the Coffin Thirteen while Postell keeps his finger in Alto's politics and gets rich fleecin' the boys here in the Blue Casino. If yuh're a gamblin' man, Field, don't do none of it in this place. Yuh'll buck crooked wheels an' cold decks everywhere yuh turn. The Blue Casino is strictly for the transient trade."

Hatfield eyed Jepp Vozar with casual interest. The Coffin 13 foreman was a half-breed, judging from his shoulder-long mane of black hair and his swarthy skin, and he had powerful shoulders. The curved grips of twin six-guns jutted from Vozar's flanks like plow handles and, from where Hatfield sat, he could count a dozen notches on the back straps of Vozar's .45s.

Playing opposite Vozar at the poker table was a seedy-looking little man with a crop of white whiskers that reached to his waist. He wore a battered sombrero and a parfleche jacket.

"Smoky Joe, the prospector," Rome identified the old man, noting the direction of Hatfield's stare. "Mines gold over in the Corazones. Comes to Alto about twice a year for supplies, usin' gold dust for money. Likes to buck the tiger and get drunk here at the Blue Casino before he gets astraddle his jenny mule and heads back across the basin."

A third poker player at the table, seated between Smoky Joe and the houseman who was dealing, attracted Hatfield's attention now by lifting an arm to signal Grote Postell over to the table.

"You tell that Zolanda gal I wanted to see her Hat Dance?" the man inquired, as Postell stepped up, grinning affably.

"That I did, Duke," Postell chuckled. "She'll be on stage as soon as she can get into that cut-down costume you boys pay to see."

Hatfield eyed the "Red Duke" with interest. On the surface, he appeared to be one of the wastrel foreigners who were occasionally seen in the West—a British remittance man, perhaps a man who actually had the title of duke back in the old country, but who had taken on Western ways, even to the drawled speech.

The Red Duke was dressed foppishly in a white shirt, black string tie, and neatly tailored gray suit. A rattlesnake band adorned his expensive El Stroud sombrero, and his pliable fingers betrayed recent manicuring as he deftly shoved chips into the pot. A half-empty whisky bottle was at the Red Duke's elbow, and he was obviously more than a little drunk.

Hatfield wondered vaguely if the Red Duke was courting Zolanda Ruiz.

The batwings fanned open and Hatfield turned to see a tall, stoop-shouldered man enter the Blue Casino. On his suspender strap a tin star was pinned.

"Vic Drumm," Rome's whisper came right on cue in Hatfield's ear. "Sheriff of Thundergust County. If yuh're on the dodge, yuh got to pay Drumm enough to keep him from gettin' interested in the bounty yuh carry on yore topknot."

Hatfield made no comment, satisfied to let his employer ticket him for an outlaw hiding out in Alto. He was glad to get this information about Vic Drumm from an unbiased citizen of the town like Sam Rome, for it warned him not to trust the local sheriff in case of a showdown.

If Les Radley was known as a wanted smuggler here in Alto—which was not at all unlikely—then Radley was probably paying tribute to the sheriff. As Vic Drumm threaded through the crowd toward the bar, Hatfield unconsciously likened him to a vulture in quest of prey.

A stir of interest at Jepp Vozar's poker table brought Hatfield's attention back to the game in progress there. A sizable pot was on the baize. The dealer and the Red Duke had dropped out of the betting and had thrust their hands into the discard. The contest was now between the Coffin 13 ramrod and the old desert rat, "Smoky Joe."

"I'll see that and raise you," Smoky Joe sang out, fishing inside his jacket for a buckskin poke. "There's ten ounces of dust in this sack, Vozar. Nineteen bucks an ounce at the current exchange. That'll take a stack of blues if'n yuh want to see what I got."

Hatfield stood up to get a better view of the hands. Vozar had two red aces and two treys in sight. Smoky Joe was raising on an ace of spades, two black eights and a queen of diamonds.

On the table, Vozar had the old prospector beat. The payoff would be decided by their respective hole cards.

"Watch Smoky Joe get tooken," Sam Rome chuckled in Hatfield's ear. "He can't play stud any better'n I can."

Hatfield saw Vozar tug at his lower lip, then thrust a stack of blues into the pot.

"I'll see yuh," grumbled the Coffin 13 foreman.

Smoky Joe scanned the crowd assembled around the table with a sparky blue eye. Chuckling, the old desert rat flipped his hole card—to reveal the ace of clubs.

The Red Duke wiped his fingers with a silk handkerchief and took a swig at his bottle of rye.

"The dead man's hand—black aces and eights!" chuckled the fop. "Unless yuh got a trey in the hole to make a full house, Vozar, the old galoot's two pair will beat yuh."

Jepp Vozar's lips moved on an oath as he boxed his cards and thrust them into the discard.

"I'm beat," he grumbled. "It's a lucky thing you wasn't dealin' this round, Smoky, or I'd nail yore hide on a fence for cold-decking me."

Smoky Joe scooped the winnings into his hat, and stood up to announce his withdrawal from the game.

"Quittin' while yuh're ahead, yuh cheap tinhorn?" demanded Vozar, his voice rising on a note of anger.

Smoky Joe started elbowing his way toward the cashier's cage to cash in his chips.

"Don't play to lose," he retorted.

Smoky Joe left the Casino, considerably more wealthy than when he had entered. Hatfield, relaxing in his chair while he waited for Zolanda Ruiz to appear on the stage, noted that Jepp Vozar had come to his feet and was signaling one of Postell's white-jacketed Mexican floormen to his side.

Vozar whispered something to the Mexican, who nodded and headed out the door by which Smoky Joe had made his departure. Then Vozar sat down at the table, called for a new deck and settled himself for the next round.

"Five gets yuh fifty that Smoky Joe don't get out of town with Vozar's *dinero*," Sam Rome commented. "I got a hunch Jepp didn't send Primotivo Freitas out for a schooner of beer."

The dealer was calling for another player to take Smoky Joe's chair and Sam Rome, ignoring the advice he had given the Lone Wolf, hastened over to buy in the game.

Rome's judgment regarding Vozar's instructions to Freitas, the floorman, had coincided exactly with Hatfield's own hunch. Freitas had been dispatched to waylay the whiskered old desert rat and seize his poker winnings.

Always alert to help an underdog, Jim Hatfield rose from his chair and stepped out on the Casino porch. He was in time to see Primotivo Freitas' white-jacketed figure duck into an alley between Rome's livery stable and the gunsmith's shop adjoining it.

Swiftly the Lone Wolf crossed the street and headed into the same alley.

Out at the rear of the livery stable, the prospector was engaged in cinching a battered stock saddle on a flop-eared jenny mule, preparatory to returning to his mining claim over in the Corazones.

Even as Jim Hatfield entered the alley, he saw the Blue Casino houseman close in on the unsuspecting oldster from the rear, a shot-loaded blackjack clutched in one fist.

Before the Ranger could shout a warning to the old man, Freitas' bludgeon clubbed across Smoky Joe's skull and the prospector wilted at his mule's feet, knocked cold by the treacherous blow.

With swift skill, Freitas reached under Smoky Joe's leather jacket and took out the miner's poke. Then, lifting a ten-inch bowie knife from its sheath at his belt, Freitas lifted the razor-honed *cuchillo* for a stabbing blow at his victim's ribs.

CHAPTER VII

Bounty-Hunting Sheriff

The entire length of the livery barn separated Jim Hatfield from the spot where a killing was about to be committed.

Snapping his Colt from holster, the Ranger thumbed off a shot, saw his bullet smash into Freitas' knife arm. It was long range for a gun Hatfield had never used before; and he was realistic enough to know that luck had been with him. But he had only wounded Freitas, and the Mexican was doubtlessly armed.

With a bellow of agony, Freitas dropped the bowie knife and stared for an instant at his bleeding wrist. Then he whirled, dropping the gold poke into a pocket of his white jacket.

"*Maños altos!*" Hatfield yelled, charging forward with smoke wisping from the rusty barrel of his Colt.

Freitas snarled a Spanish oath and his right hand stabbed under the lapel of his white jacket. Sunlight flashed on gun metal as the Mexican brought a six-gun into the open and squeezed trigger.

The bullet ricocheted off the stable wall and smashed out a window pane in the gunsmith's shop alongside Hatfield's shoulder. Flinging himself to the ground to reduce his vulnerability as a target, Hatfield tripped his gun hammer, cursed as the firing pin clicked on a defective cartridge.

Freitas was leveling his gun for another shot now. A breath before he pulled trigger, the Ranger rolled swiftly to one side, and Freitas' second bullet churned into the dusty alley where Hatfield had been lying.

Twirling the cylinder of his Colt, the Lone Wolf notched his gunsights on Freitas just as the Mexican leaped to put the corner of the livery barn between him and his attacker. The gun bucked against the crotch of Hatfield's thumb and founting gunsmoke momentarily blocked the Ranger's view. When it cleared, he saw Primotivo Freitas' legs sprawled around the corner of the barn, his heels beating a sharp tattoo on the adobe.

The thunder of gunshots, amplified by the walls of the alley buildings, had attracted the attention of the town. Vaguely Hatfield was aware of men shouting on the street behind him, of boots thudding out of the Blue Casino to investigate.

He came to his feet, reloading his smoking gun. Freitas' threshing legs were still now.

Taking no chances of running into a trap, Hatfield headed down the alley, his shoulder rubbing the board-and-bat wall of Rome's barn. Men were racing down the alley behind him as he reached the corner of the barn and saw that his second bullet had gone home. Blood was guttering from a hole drilled through Freitas' hairy temple. The slug had lodged in the Mexican's brain, killing him instantly.

Ignoring the babbling throng which was gathering, Hatfield strode over to Smoky Joe's mule and unhooked a canteen from the pommel. He unscrewed the cap and sloshed the brackish contents of the canteen over the prospector's bald skull, where a livid welt was swelling to the dimensions of a goose egg.

Scanning the crowd, Jim Hatfield recognized several faces he had seen in the Blue Casino. Jepp Vozar was staring at him with grim hatred, his glance swinging over to regard the dead Mexican.

At Vozar's shoulder was the Red Duke, looking even more out of place in this rough-dressed assemblage because of his smooth-shaven, well-groomed appearance. Swaying drunkenly on his feet, the Red Duke was laughing foolishly, unconcerned by the fact that he had witnessed the aftermath of a bloody shoot-out.

Bending over Freitas' corpse was the fustian-coated figure of the town boss, Grote Postell. The man was puffing savagely at his Cuban cigar as he looked up.

"Yuh've killed my best floorman, stranger. Yuh'll swing for this . . . Where's the sheriff?"

An aisle cleared in the group of spectators jamming the alley and the stooped, scrawny figure of Vic Drumm emerged from the press, the sun flashing on his sheriff's star. A gun was in Drumm's hand as he swung his pale, baleful eyes on Hatfield.

"Killed a man in broad daylight, eh?" snarled the lawman, reaching in his levis pocket for a pair of handcuffs. "Yuh're comin' to the lock-up with me, son."

Hatfield holstered his gun and held up a restraining hand as the Alto sheriff approached him.

"Hold on a second, Drumm!" he snapped. "All of you folks, listen to what I got to say. Let me show yuh a few things."

Hatfield pointed to Freitas' blackjack lying in the dust, then to the bruises on Smoky Joe's head. The old desert rat was stirring, and moaning feebly as consciousness returned.

"Take it from the beginnin', men," Hatfield said desperately. "Old Smoky Joe here won a sizable poker pot from Vozar yonder. Right after Smoky Joe left the Casino, Freitas trailed him. I saw him slug the old-timer with that blackjack."

Hatfield stooped to pick up the Mexican's knife.

"Freitas robbed Smoky Joe of his poke and was fixed to stab him to death," the Ranger went on. "I put a slug through Freitas' left arm, to save Joe's life. Then Freitas' hauled a gun and started shootin' at me. I can show yuh where his bullet glanced off the barn wall and went into the gunshop window."

There was a moment's silence following Hatfield's recital. Grote Postell, still kneeling beside the dead body of his Casino floor man, spoke up harshly.

"Anybody see all this happen, stranger? How do we know you wasn't tryin' to rob the old prospector and that Primo caught yuh at it?"

Hatfield grinned without mirth. He was only a couple of tricks away from being the victim of a lynch mob, he knew. The victim of this shooting scrape might be only a Mexican saloon swamper, but he was one of Grote Postell's employees and that loomed big in the eyes of this town.

"Take a look in Freitas' pocket," Hatfield invited the crowd. "See what yuh find there!"

Postell hesitated, then rummaged in the Mexican's white jacket. He drew out a greasy leather sack from which came the chinking sound of gold specie which the Blue Casino's cashier had exchanged for Smoky Joe's poker chips.

"Just a minute," growled Sheriff Vic Drumm, eyeing Hatfield truculently. "Who are you? I never seen yuh around town before."

All eyes were focused on Jim Hatfield again, and the Ranger's brows drew together in a worried frown. At all costs, he wanted to keep his identity secret in this outlaw town. There was too much at stake for him to risk revealing the Ranger badge he kept hidden in a secret compartment of his chaps belt.

"Answer the sheriff's question, stranger!" ordered Grote Postell.

Hatfield licked his lips. "My name's Jim Field," he said. "I'm just a tumbleweed puncher, headin' for Thundergust Basin with the idea of rentin' my lass'-rope at some cow outfit. I've never been in Alto before today."

The sheriff's beady eyes narrowed. A self-confessed bounty-hunter, Vic Drumm was wondering if this stranger's picture was on file in his collection of reward posters.

"Field works for me, Sheriff!" spoke up a new voice, and grizzled old Sam Rome elbowed his way to the front of the crowd. "He's my new night man. And it's my fault this happened."

Vic Drumm whirled to face the owner of the Tombstone Trail Livery. Rome was an old-timer in Alto, a man whose word was not to be thrust aside without due consideration.

"What yuh mean, Freitas' killin' is yore fault, Sam?" growled the sheriff belligerently. "Yuh know what yuh're sayin'?"

Sam Rome scuffed the dirt with his boot toe. Off to one side, Smoky Joe was grabbing his mule's stirrup and dragging himself to his feet, groggy from the effects of his skull injury.

"I saw Vozar tip off the Mexican to foller Smoky Joe," Rome said, with a flare of courage which brought a grin of thanksgiving to Hatfield's lips. "Field tailed Primo. I'm believin' Field killed the Mexican in self-defense."

Strangely enough, it was Jepp Vozar who came to Hatfield's aid in this tense moment.

"Let 'im go, Sheriff," grumbled the Coffin 13 foreman. "I admit sendin' Primotivo out to get my *dinero* back from the old man. I was likkered up and didn't know what I was doin'. But I didn't aim for Freitas to stab Smoky Joe."

Vic Drumm holstered his gun and pocketed his handcuffs. He gestured to two men in the crowd.

"Haul Primo's carcass over to the coroner's," he bit out. "You, Field—watch yore step in this town as long as I'm ramroddin' it. Yuh're lucky yuh didn't stretch hemp for this killin'."

Confusion milled around Hatfield as the sheriff turned to go. Two men picked up Freitas' corpse and set off down the alley with it. Grote Postell handed Smoky Joe his bag of specie and, linking his arm through Vozar's, set off in the direction of the Blue Casino. As the crowd broke up, Hatfield found himself alone with Sam Rome and Smoky Joe.

"Thanks, Boss." The Ranger grinned, shaking Rome's hand. "I had my tail in a tight crack and yuh unkinked it for me. Reckon I'll work for yuh for free."

Rome waggled his head somberly.

"Don't thank me," he said gruffly. "Grote Postell could have given Drumm the nod and yuh'd have been carted off to the jail with a killin' charge on yuh. I reckon Postell had reasons for slippin' Vozar the signal to call off the sheriff's dogs."

Rome crawled through the corral fence and disappeared into the back of his livery barn, badly shaken by what he had seen and his own risky rôle in coming to the stranger's defense.

Hatfield turned to see Smoky Joe regarding him dazedly.

"I won't forget what yuh done for me, young feller," the desert rat said thickly. "I'm in yore debt from now till hell freezes over. Ary time yuh get over across the basin, yuh'll find me workin' a placer claim over in Lava-rock Canyon. I'll cut yuh in on shares to pay yuh back for savin' my worthless hide."

Hatfield laughed, holding the mule's bridle while the old prospector mounted.

"Forget it, Dad," the Ranger chuckled. "Yuh'd have done the same for me, I reckon."

When the old prospector rode away, Jim Hatfield went over to the telegraph office. There he composed an innocent-sounding message to a certain individual in Presidio, Clint Jackson, telling him that he was remaining in Alto and wanted his horse brought to Sam Rome's stables.

Clint Jackson was a pseudonym for the Texas Ranger in charge of the Presidio office, and the telegram, signed "Field," would tip off the Ranger official that the Lone Wolf's man-hunt trail was temporarily focused on Thundergust Basin.

After paying the Overland Telegraph operator, Hatfield stepped back onto Main Street and turned toward the Alto House, intending to get lodgings there. Then, remembering his promise to watch Zolanda Ruiz' song and dance act, he retraced his steps to the Blue Casino.

A buzz of excitement went through Postell's establishment as men recognized Hatfield. For the Ranger, this notoriety was the worst possible thing that could have happened. He had hoped to remain an obscure figure in the background of the town's daily tempo, keeping an eye out for Les Radley's possible appearance.

Now he found himself a marked man, a stranger with a killer rep, a man who had slain one of Grote Postell's saloon crew and who, therefore, would be a target for

Postell's reprisal. Worse, he had drawn Jepp Vozar into making a public confession of trying to rob Smoky Joe, the prospector, of his fairly-won poker stake All in all, it added up to a situation which was fraught with danger for a lone Texas Ranger in a hostile town.

CHAPTER VIII

Red Duke Apologizes

Jim Hatfield found a bench near the saloon's stage, ordered a drink from a cruising floor man and settled down to wait for Zolanda's belated appearance.

The stage footlight had been turned up to maximum brilliance and the colored pianist had been joined by a Mexican with his *maracas* and a tom-tom, a fiddle player, and a bartender who played a guitar.

The orchestra struck up the stirring strains of "La Paloma," a backstage snare drummer played a crescendoing roll, and cymbals clanged behind the curtain.

Then the curtains were yanked apart and the barroom crowd stamped feet and bawled lusty approval of the giant, six-foot-crowned Mexican sombrero which occupied the center of the stage. The orchestra went into a lively fandango rhythm and from the wings Zolanda Ruiz pirouetted with a swirl of skirts and a dry clatter of castanets.

Hatfield applauded with the others as the Mexican *damosela* went into her whirling dance, high heels clicking the rhythm of the exotic "Hat Dance," whirling herself around and around the mammoth sombrero with ever-increasing speed.

When the wild, mad Mexican dance had finished, Zolanda took her bows at stage center, beads of perspiration shining on her olive forehead in the glare of the guttering lamps. Her sweeping gaze picked out Jim

Hatfield in the audience and a message flashed between them.

Finally, tucking her castanets into her satin sash, Zolanda raised her bejeweled arms for quiet.

"*Muchas gracias, señores!*" her musical voice came over the crowd, short of breath from her exertion. "You are ver' kind. And now, I seeng for you gentlemens. Do I hear thos' requasts, *si?*"

A cowboy in the rear of the hall shouted, "Buffalo Gals!" at the top of his lungs. Other patrons of the Blue Casino yelled their choices. Finally, above the cacophony, a man leaped up on a table and, brandishing a whisky bottle, squalled lustily:

"The Hat Dance! Give me the Hat Dance ag'in, Zolanda!"

The dancing girl frowned and shook her head. Turning, Jim Hatfield saw that this request came from the remittance man known as the Red Duke. Completely tipsy now, the Red Duke hurled his whisky bottle at the stage, shattering it on the wood-and-canvas sombrero prop.

Hatfield scowled at this display, thinking that one of Postell's bouncers would descend on the Red Duke and escort him bodily out of the saloon. Instead, the crowd roared with mirth and started applauding.

Zolanda signaled the Negro pianist and the orchestra went into "*La Golondrina.*" The Red Duke climbed down off the table and sat glowering at the stage as the pandemonium subsided and the Mexican girl started singing the plaintive love song about the swallow.

Jim Hatfield's memory sped back across the gulf of years since he had last seen Zolanda's act, and sadness laid its edge against his spirit. Something was lacking from her voice, which once had had the power to hold men in its magic spell.

The resonance was gone from her throaty contralto. The heartbreak, while it blended with the sad words of the Spanish lyric, went far beyond a songstress' histrionics; it was a genuine pathos, hinting of the suffering which Les Radley had brought to this woman in the past.

When her song was finished, Zolanda acknowledged the tumultuous applause of the Casino's patrons and descended the stage steps to mingle with the crowd. She purposely avoided Jim Hatfield's corner, for which the Lone Wolf was grateful. This town must not know that they had known each other in the past, however briefly.

As Zolanda seated herself at a table with several cowhands from the Coffin 13 spread, the Red Duke left his table and zigzagged his way toward her.

"I paid fifty dollarsh for the Hat Dansh!" bellowed the foppishly-dressed sport. "I didn' get my money'sh worth. You dansh ag'in, Zolanda, or I'll busht yore purty neck for yuh!"

Knots of muscle grated in the corners of Jim Hatfield's jaw as he waited for the reaction of the men in the saloon to this brazen conduct on the part the Red Duke.

But the crowd was already beginning to head back for the bar and the gaming tables, Zolanda's mid-afternoon entertainment having come to a close. Stage hands drew the theater curtains and the orchestra retired for an intermission.

"Senor," Zolanda said to the Red Duke as he reached her table, "the Hat Dance ees ver' difficult. *Esta noche*—tonight—I dance eet for you *ademas*, no?"

The Red Duke reached down and locked a fist around Zolanda's slim wrist, hauling her roughly to her feet. The Coffin 13 cowpunchers made no move to intervene.

"You dansh now, savvy?" roared the Red Duke. "I paid Grote Poshtell fifty bucksh to see you dansh, an' by gosh you'll dansh till I tell you to shtop, savvy?"

Jim Hatfield came to his feet, his hands fisting angrily. He saw Zolanda jerk herself free of the Duke's grasp, and, stepping back, slap the man a stinging blow across the cheek.

"No!" she shrilled. "*Caramba*, no! I am *muy fatigado*, very tired. I cannot dance thos' Sombrero Fandango weethout I geet the rest!"

The Red Duke bawled an oath and, hauling back a manicured hand, lashed it savagely across her jaw. Zolanda staggered under the blow and, tripping, fell into the arms of Jim Hatfield.

Helping the girl to her feet, the Lone Wolf Ranger caught Zolanda's anxious whisper:

"No, Senor Jeem! Do nothing! The Duke ees dangerous when he ees dronk."

But anger had seized Hatfield now, outrage at this man-handling of a woman. Helping her into the chair he had vacated, the Ranger turned and stalked across the floor to where the Red Duke stood, swaying on his feet.

"What kind of a town is this," raged Hatfield, staring around at the circle of faces, "where a dude can rough up a woman without a man liftin' a hand to help?"

It was deathly quiet in the Blue Casino now. Through the tail of his eye, Hatfield saw Grote Postell and the sheriff edging along the wall toward the stage.

"Jim Field, the tough buckaroo from nowhere!" rasped the Duke, rubbing his palms up and down his foxed California pants. "Lookin' for trouble, Field? Unbuckle that killer's hogleg yuh wear and I'll show yuh if I'm a dude!"

Hatfield unbuckled his shell-belt and laid his gun on the piano top, his lips white with anger. The Red Duke might be drunk, but not too drunk to know what he was doing.

Sheriff Vic Drumm closed in between the Ranger and the Duke, shaking his head and frowning.

"Keep yore horns out of this business, Field!" snapped the lawman. "Yuh've already hogged yore share of the spotlight since yuh hit these diggin's. What's Zolanda to you?"

Hatfield turned his angry eyes on the sheriff.

"She's a woman, mauled by a man twice her size. If you had any nerve yuh'd clap the Red Duke in jail for disturbin' the peace, Drumm."

The Red Duke stepped forward, shoving Drumm to one side.

"Field asked for trouble, Vic," snarled the Duke. "I'm the man who can clean his plow."

Vic Drumm moved swiftly around behind Hatfield then, reaching out to cinch a bear-hug around the Ranger, pinning his arms to his sides. The Duke, seizing his opportunity, lunged in with a looping haymaker which cracked against Hatfield's jaw with a meaty impact which made fireworks explode in the Ranger's brain.

Berserk with rage, Hatfield broke the sheriff's grip and ducked an uppercut which the Duke launched at his head. Before Drumm could intervene, the Ranger had danced to one side and landed a jolting one-two to the Duke's stomach and heart.

Wincing with pain, cold sober now, the Red Duke fell back a pace, shook his head to clear it, then stripped off his form-fitting gray coat, rolled up his sleeves to reveal white but well-muscled forearms, and squared off like a professional boxer to meet Hatfield's next rush.

Before they had exchanged half a dozen punches, Hatfield knew that he was facing a trained pugilist, a deadly pair of fists. But Hatfield could fight with murderous effectiveness when the chips were down, and he went to work now with a cold fury which made him impervious to the Red Duke's lancing jabs.

Carrying the fight to the Duke, the Lone Wolf launched an assault of slugging lefts and rights which chopped the Duke's smile off his face, sealed up one eye, opened a cut over the Duke's right cheek bone. Hammering with abandon, punching through the Duke's defenses, outmatching his footwork, Jim Hatfield drove the Duke against the piano, slugged him the length of the stage, and pinned him against the wall.

Dazed and bleeding, the Red Duke sagged to his knees and covered his face with his hands, bewildered by the unleashed leonine savagery of Hatfield's attack. With a cold snarl, the Ranger hauled the Duke to his feet while the crowd closed in, baying for the kill, the pay-off punch.

"Yuh'll apologize to Senorita Ruiz," Hatfield panted, "and then yuh'll get out of this barroom."

The fight had been brief and devastating. The Red

Duke, who had never been bested in a barroom brawl before this, had been beaten into submission by a man whom he outweighed and outreached. He spat out a tooth and moaned.

"All right—all right!" he gasped. "You win this round, Field."

The Red Duke staggered over to where Zolanda Ruiz had been a petrified witness of the slugging match.

"I apologize, Zolanda," he said hoarsely. "I—I'll never ask yuh to dance for me ag'in."

With that, the Red Duke picked up his coat and lurched off, to lose himself in the crowd that had witnessed his humiliation. In the Red Duke—whether he was gambler, business man or outlaw, Hatfield did not know—the Ranger had made a mortal enemy, one who might bide his time to strike back from ambush.

Zolanda flung Hatfield a look that was a blend of terror and gratitude, gathered up her skirts and vanished behind the stage proscenium. The Lone Wolf, suddenly weary, and realizing his own drained forces, crossed over to the piano and reclaimed his gun.

He was engaged in buckling the shell-studded belt around his lean midriff when Grote Postell approached him, the fragrant aroma of his perfecto telegraphing the saloonman's presence behind him. Hatfield turned, ready for fresh trouble, only to see glinting approval mirrored in Postell's gooseberry-green eyes.

"Yuh've cut yoreself a wide swath in this town, young man." Postell grinned. "Killed one of my best *mozos*, and beat up a man who was once a professional prize-fighter in England. I congratulate yuh, Jim Field. And I advise yuh to enjoy life while you can. It will be a short life, I'm afraid."

The Ranger adjusted the Colt at his his hip and stared back.

"Is that a threat or a warning?" he asked. "Or both?"

Grote Postell studied the tip of his cigar abstractly.

"Call it a friendly warnin'. However, I can sell yuh some guaranteed life insurance, senor."

"Meanin' I should leave town while I can?" Hatfield

grunted sarcastically. "No dice, Postell. I've got myself a job. I'm stickin' around till I can get me a grubstake."

Postell returned the perfecto to his gold-capped teeth.

"Not at all. I am invitin' yuh to work for me, young man. No enemy will bother yuh if yuh're known as a Postell gun-toter. And the pay is high. Five hundred a month and found—in return for obeyin' to the letter whatever orders I send yore way."

The Lone Wolf fashioned himself a brownie cigarette and pondered Grote Postell's lavish offer. The Coffin 13 cattle king had sized up Hatfield for a tough customer, apparently, and Hatfield resolved to live up to that appraisal now.

"Half a thousand a month," he echoed. "Yuh must be hirin' me for duty outside the law, at that figger."

Postell shrugged. "Are yuh particular, Field?"

The Ranger grinned.

"I'll think over yore offer," he temporized. "Right now, I'm dead for sleep. See yuh later, senor."

CHAPTER IX

Rafter B Wrangler

Renting a room in the Alto House, Hatfield washed up in a zinc tub behind the cowtown hostelry, then donned a new shirt and bibless levis which the clerk had purchased for him with Sam Rome's money at a local mercantile store. Going upstairs, Hatfield turned in and was asleep the moment his head hit the pillow.

The clerk roused him in time for supper, and sundown found him reporting at the Tombstone Trail Livery, much refreshed by his four-hour sleep. He found Sam Rome waiting for him.

"Yore first job will be to curry that palomino in the front stall yonder," Rome told his new hand. "That belongs to the Red Duke, and he'll be in after his nag later tonight. Make shore yuh don't let him pick a fight with yuh—or catch yuh with yore back turned."

Hatfield smiled. "I won't quarrel with yore cash customers, Rome," he promised. "This Red Duke—who is he? Cuts a wide splash locally, or is he just a saloon barfly?"

Rome muttered an oath. "Remittance man—ne'er-do-well from Cornwall, they say. Ramrods one of the smaller cow spreads in the basin as a hobby. Watch him close, Field. He's dangerous. He's proud. A bad man to have for an enemy, especially after the thrashin' yuh give him in public today."

Hatfield thanked the livery man for his warning and started his chores. The night was well along by the time he had bedded down the stock, washed several sets of harness, and soaped a couple of Coffin 13 saddles.

This job at Rome's barn satisfied his purpose exactly. The only stable in Alto, it gave Hatfield a chance to size up any horsemen who stabled their mounts overnight. And, working the night shift, it left him free to scout the town daytimes.

Grote Postell's lucrative offer to rent his gun piqued the Lone Wolf's interest. With an uncanny knack for sizing up owlhooters, a skill bred of his years behind a Ranger badge, Hatfield believed that it might be worth his while to probe into Grote Postell's activities carefully, during his stay here.

The Rangers were embarked on a long-range program to wipe out the rustling gangs and smuggler bands which plied their illicit commerce on the Tombstone Trail, and it was quite possible that Postell had a finger in this traffic. If so, Hatfield's sojourn in Alto might prove far more important than his original purpose of lying in wait here on the chance that Les Radley would show up in town.

Well after midnight, the Blue Casino closed its doors. Up until two o'clock, business was brisk for Jim Field, as men called for their saddle horses and wagon teams. But when Alto finally settled down for the night, the Red Duke's leggy palomino remained unclaimed in its stall. The Duke, apparently, had elected to remain in town overnight.

It was shortly before dawn when Hatfield, dozing in Rome's front office, was roused by a visitor. In the clotted gloom he had difficulty at first in recognizing Zolanda Ruiz.

"Yuh shouldn't be here, *niña!*" Hatfield said impatiently. "Get back to yore room!"

The Mexican dancing girl clung to his wrist.

"I—I wanted to thank you for what you did for me, Senor Jeem," she whispered anxiously. "And I want to warn you not to let another sundown find you een Alto. I have a feeling you weel not be alive for long eef you remain here."

Hatfield scowled in the darkness.

"Why? Has Les Radley showed up since I saw yuh?"

Zolanda shook her head.

"No. Eef he does, I would tell you *pronto prontico.* No. The sheriff hates you, Jeem. He theenks you are an outlaw. Thos' *malo hombre,* the Red Duke, he weel keel you first chance he gets. And Jepp Vozar ees your *enimigo.* I am afraid for your life, Jeem."

Hatfield laughed gently in the darkness.

"For a peace-lovin' gent who wanted to keep to himself," he said ironically, "I've shore collected myself a bunch of ill-wishers my first day in town, haven't I?"

Zolanda left shortly, failing to shake Hatfield's inflexible decision to remain in Alto. An hour after sunup, Sam Rome's daytime hostler came to relieve him.

Hatfield breakfasted at the Alto House and, still behind in his sleep, went up to his room, locked the door and went to bed. . . .

Hunger pangs awakened him at three o'clock that afternoon. Leaving the hotel after a hearty meal, intending to stroll the length of main street and better acquaint himself with the details of this mountain town, Hatfield caught sight of a Conestoga wagon drawn up in front of the O.K. Mercantile. Painted on the box of the heavy wagon was a Rafter B brand, and the same iron marked the rumps of the six-horse team hitched to the vehicle.

"The Rafter B," Hatfield mused. "That'll be Beth Beloud's outfit across the basin. I wonder—"

He angled across the street and watched a husky young redhead busy trundling sacks of chicken feed, reels of barbed wire, and other supplies from the mercantile store, loading them in the high-boxed wagon.

When the red-headed waddy paused to unroll a canvas tarp to cover his load, Hatfield approached him and asked for a match.

"You work at the Rafter B, feller?" he asked.

The redhead nodded, dragging a sleeve across his ruddy face.

"That's right. Name's Dall Stockton. I'm the cavvy wrangler."

Making no offer to introduce himself, Hatfield said casually:

"I know yore boss, Miss Beloud. She come back since her father was bushwhacked?"

Dall Stockton nodded. "Got back yesterday. Her stage was wrecked comin' down from Fort Davis, in that storm. She hoofed it over the Rosillos."

Hatfield grinned his relief. He was glad to know that Beth was safe at home following her ordeal, at any rate.

"Matter of fact," Stockton went on, glancing up and down the street, "Beth rode into town with me this mornin'. She's scoutin' around for Leon Hesterling right now."

"Hesterling?" the Ranger echoed.

Stockton made a grimace and spat into the dust.

"Hesterling's the Rafter B foreman. And the hombre who's goin' to own the spread after he marries Beth. At which time I aim to draw my time and skedaddle."

Leaving Stockton at his work in front of the Mercantile, Hatfield strolled on past the Blue Casino. He caught sight of Zolanda Ruiz leaning from her bedroom window upstairs. She gave him the briefest of head-shakes, which told him that, so far as she was concerned, Les Radley had not made an appearance in Alto.

Hatfield strolled on up the street, his eyes fixed on the remote blue haze of Thundergust Basin. The gray ribbon of the Tombstone Trail lay arrow-straight across the flats, vanishing in the rugged spurs of the Corazone Range on its way to the Rio Grande crossing.

The Ranger stepped off the road to make way for an inbound Well's-Fargo stage. He was seated on a rock by the roadside, at the extreme fringe of the town, when he heard a thud of hoofbeats through the dust and the whinny of a horse which set his pulses racing.

Peering through the dust of the Concord's passage, Hatfield saw a horse and rider approaching from the direction of Thundergust Basin. Trailing the rider was a magnificent golden sorrel gelding, rigged with a high-horned Brazos saddle.

"Goldy!" Hatfield exclaimed, getting to his feet.

It was like greeting an old friend, seeing his horse again. Indeed, Goldy was the best friend Jim Hatfield could boast. More than once in his danger-checkered career as a Texas lawman, this leggy, prancing sorrel had saved his life. There was a rapport between man and animal which was rarely achieved even between human friends.

Shifting his gaze from the sorrel, Hatfield recognized the rider on the claybank stallion. It was "Buddy" Ingalls, a new rookie on Roaring Bill McDowell's Ranger troop, currently stationed at the Presidio district headquarters for training.

Ingalls, then, was the Ranger who had been assigned the job of bringing Hatfield his mount, in response to his telegram. The husky young Irish rookie was not wearing his Ranger star. To all appearances, he was a drifting saddle bum, and a thoroughly trail-weary tumbleweed at that. His claybanker was limping and hoofsore, and even Goldy showed the strain of a long fast trek across the Big Bend.

"Howdy, stranger," Ingalls greeted Hatfield. "Could yuh tell me where I could find a good livery barn?"

For the benefit of a pair of passing cowpunchers whose mounts bore Coffin 13 brands, the Lone Wolf answered loudly:

"Tombstone Trail Livery is the only stable in town, busky."

Ingalls reined up and hipped around in saddle, letting Goldy's hackamore go slack. The deep-chested gelding nuzzled Jim Hatfield affectionately after his two-week's absence from his rider. For various reasons, Hatfield had gone into the Paisano Pass country after Les Radley on foot rather than on horseback.

"Had to ride all night to make it, Jim," Ingalls said, twisting a cigarette. "Anything yuh want me to report?"

Hatfield, ostensibly engrossed in the job of rolling a smoke for himself, said in a guarded undertone:

"Have yore chief telegraph Roaring Bill McDowell over in Austin that I'm stickin' around Alto for a while. May get a line on the Tombstone Trail smugglers. Tell him that Les Radley slipped out of my loop, but that I expect to rearrest him before long."

Ingalls clucked his tongue sympathetically.

"Sorry to hear about Radley. What'll I do with Goldy?"

Hatfield jerked his thumb toward the town.

"Stable him at the livery barn and pay for a couple weeks' groomin' and grainin' in advance. If yuh see me around town, don't recognize me. I'm playin' things close to the vest here."

Ingalls picked up his reins, nodding doubtfully. He eyed the shabby-looking gun at Hatfield's flank.

"Shore I can't be of help on this deal? I'd be glad to stick around and back yore play if yuh get crowded into a tight."

Hatfield shook his head. "*Muchas gracias,* Buddy. No. I'll play it solo."

The fledgling Ranger laughed softly. "Always the Lone Wolf, eh, Jim?" he said, and spurred on toward Alto, leading Goldy at the end of a trail rope.

After an interval, Hatfield returned to the Alto House and went upstairs to his room. He felt better, knowing that his extra pair of Colt six-guns were waiting for him in Goldy's saddle-bags. He had felt ill at ease ever since Les Radley had appropriated his guns.

Hatfield was sitting at his bedroom window, sizing up the passing traffic on the main street below him, when a knock sounded at his door. Loosening his gun in holster, the Lone Wolf strode over to the door and opened it.

Standing in the hotel corridor was a slim girl in an apricot-colored rodeo blouse, split-type riding skirt and taffy-brown cowboots. A snow-white Stetson was held against the back of her shoulders by a pleated chin-strap. In the dim light of the hall, it was a moment before Hatfield recognized his visitor as the girl he had saved from the stagecoach wreck on Tornillo Creek.

"Miss Beloud!" Hatfield said courteously then, stepping to one side as she entered. "I'm glad to see yuh're safe and sound."

CHAPTER X

Beth's Dilemma

Beth Beloud shook Hatfield's proffered hand, and he sensed that she was trembling, fighting to keep herself under control.

"Mr. Radley," she said hoarsely, "I'm in trouble. I need help, and need it desperately. So as a—as a last resort, I have come to you."

Nodding gravely, Jim Hatfield drew up a chair for the girl and sat down on his bed facing her. She was twisting a red bandanna neckerchief between her fingers, and he saw that her eyes were swollen and red-rimmed from recent weeping.

Remembering the courage she had displayed during their ordeal in the Tornillo, it struck him that it must be some great tragedy which had reduced her to tears.

"How did yuh locate me here, ma'am?" he inquired.

She colored under his gaze. "I was buying some dress goods at Mrs. Callahan's millinery shop across the street when you were talking to my cavvy wrangler, Dall Stockton. Later I saw you come in here. I asked the clerk downstairs what room you occupied."

Hatfield sat up, alarm showing in his greenish eyes.

"No, no—I didn't ask the clerk where Mr. Les Radley was staying," she amended hastily. "I described you. He knew at once who you were. Heard you called yourself Jim Field. Don't worry—your secret is safe with me, always."

Hatfield permitted himself a moment's inward amusement. Her mix-up in identification was natural enough, for both he and Les Radley had been wearing identical slickers during the ill-fated stagecoach ride, and both had been handcuffed.

Now, as before, it suited Hatfield's fancy to let her go on thinking he was an escaped outlaw, hiding out here in Alto. It was too risky to let a virtual stranger, and a girl at that, know his true identity.

"I am flattered that yuh thought I might be able to help yuh, ma'am," he drawled. "What's the trouble?"

She stared at the floor, marshaling her thoughts. Through the open window came the assorted sounds of Alto street traffic as afternoon shadows lengthened and riders began coming into town from the Basin.

"As I told you the other night," she began, "my father, Captain Robert Beloud, was killed this spring and I fell heir to the Rafter B Ranch in the Corazones foothills. There is some mystery shrouding my father's death."

She told him, then, what she knew. Old Captain Beloud had been found dead on a lonely trail back in Lavarock Canyon, his boot wedged in the stirrup of his saddle horse. Apparently he had fallen from his horse and had been dragged to his death. His body had been found by the Rafter B foreman, Leon Hesterling.

An alert county coroner, however, had insisted on making an autopsy of the dead rancher's body. His findings had revealed a .30-30 slug in Beloud's heart. The girl's father had been killed, then, and his corpse left dragging from the saddle stirrup to make it seem like an accident.

"Leon—my fiancé—is of the belief that Dad was killed by the Tombstone Trail smugglers," Beth told Hatfield bleakly. "You see, the old smuggling route goes across our Rafter B range and enters Mexico by way of Lavarock Canyon, which has an outlet on the Rio Grande. And Dad frequently patrolled Lavarock Canyon, where we have a line camp, because lots of our stock has been stolen and hazed into Mexico by way of that Canyon."

The Lone Wolf nodded somberly.

"Hesterling thinks yore father trapped a smuggler in Lavarock Canyon and was killed in the shoot-out," he said. "I see. Sounds logical. I imagine yore future husband is mebbe right about that."

Beth shook her head.

"You met my cavvy wrangler, Dall Stockton," she said. "Dall was a range orphan whose parents were killed by Comanches when he was a baby. Dad took him to raise, before I was born. I have a lot of faith in Dall's judgment. Dall doesn't believe Dad was killed by smugglers at all."

Hatfield waited for her to continue.

"Dall did some detective work after the discovery of Dad's body," she said, "and he found hoof tracks up on the rim of Lavarock Canyon, along with a thirty-thirty shell. Without boring you with details, let it be enough to say that Dall Stockton traced those hoof tracks to the Coffin Thirteen Ranch, here in Thundergust Basin. In other words, my wrangler is positive that Dad was bushwhacked by Coffin Thirteen riders. Leon scoffs at the idea. But I—I'm not sure. I don't know what to believe."

Hatfield pondered the girl's problem at some length. From what word he had picked up from conversations with Sam Rome and Zolanda Ruiz here in Alto, he knew that Grote Postell's Coffin 13 was expanding, freezing out smaller ranchers in the basin. Old Bob Beloud's Rafter B was the only small-tally outfit which had defied the Coffin 13's program to monopolize the basin graze.

"Dall Stockton is a level-headed kid," Hatfield agreed. "I have reason to believe that he is one hundred per cent loyal to the Rafter B. How do Stockton and yore foreman get along?"

Beth shook her head. "They hate each other," she said regretfully. "It—it has nothing to do with Leon's ability as a foreman. I—I guess it's because they're both in love with me. You must think me very vain to say that, but—"

Hatfield laughed. Remembering what Stockton had

said about drawing his time when Hesterling married Beth and became co-owner of the Rafter B, the Ranger was not surprised at what the girl had just told him regarding their rivalry.

"I see," he commented. "Yuh've come to me, have yuh, in the hope that I might be able to solve the mystery of yore father's killin'? Is that it?"

Beth got to her feet and made a circuit of the room. She halted in front of Hatfield, regarding him with an admixture of shame and reluctance. Whatever she had on her mind, whatever motive had impelled her to make this rendezvous with a man she believed to be a notorious outlaw in hiding, was obviously costing her plenty of embarrassment.

"No," she said finally. "Dad is dead. Nothing can bring him back. Naturally, I would like to see his killer brought to justice. But I doubt if his killing can ever be solved."

Hatfield eyed his guest with new interest. She was coming to the crux of her visit now, he sensed.

"It's about the Rafter B," she explained. "Mr. Radley, my fiancé, Dad's old foreman—Leon Hesterling—insists that I sell the ranch to Grote Postell. He says that we can't avoid bankruptcy, caught as we are between the Tombstone Trail outlaw traffic on the one hand and an expanding cattle kingdom like the Coffin Thirteen on the other."

Hatfield met her level gaze. "Has Hesterling got a buyer for the Rafter B? Has this Postell made an offer? At a respectable figure?"

Beth shrugged. "Grote Postell is after the Rafter B. No other buyer would touch it, knowing they would have to buck the Coffin Thirteen. Postell has offered us fifty thousand for the ranch, including what few shorthorns the rustlers haven't stolen. I suppose that is what anyone would call a reasonable offer."

"Then why don't you take it?"

The girl sat down heavily, grief in her eyes.

"Because Dad would rest uneasy in his grave if I sold out to Postell, his worst enemy. Dall tells me the ranch can be made to pay, if we can hire a crew that won't take to the tall timber whenever the Coffin Thirteen cuts a line fence or burns our graze."

An inkling of Beth Beloud's reason for coming to him struck Jim Hatfield now.

"Where do I come in on this deal, Miss Beloud?" he asked bluntly.

Again she showed signs of keen embarrassment.

"I—I want to hire you as the start of a new Rafter B crew," she said in a husky whisper. "You are a gunman, Mr. Radley. You would not hesitate to kill a Coffin Thirteen cowboy if you caught him blotting a brand on a Rafter B calf. Frankly, I need that kind of help. The same brand of men that Postell hires. I've got to fight fire with fire—or lose my ranch."

Jim Hatfield came to his feet, his face grimly impassive.

"I'm sorry, ma'am. My guns are not for hire."

Beth stared at him uncomprehendingly.

"But you—you have a gunman's reputation. I thought—"

Hatfield shook his head. "I've already been offered five hundred a month by Postell for that same kind of work—likely against Rafter B. I refused the Coffin Thirteen's offer. I'm refusing yores."

Tears misted Beth Beloud's lashes as she she stood up and headed for the door.

"I'm ashamed of myself for even asking you such a thing," she said with sudden violence. "Hiring killers isn't any solution for the Rafter B's troubles. Two wrongs never made a right. But I can only count on three men to back me in my fight against the Coffin Thirteen—Leon and Dall, and Wing Sing, my father's Chinese cook."

As Hatfield accompanied her to the door, he was sorely tempted to reveal his reason for refusing to help her in her back-to-the-wall struggle against the cattle baron. But the impulse passed, and he gripped the girl's hand, wishing her luck.

"You may think it is dangerous to your safety, my knowing who you are, Mr. Radley," the girl whispered.

"Please don't be worried. You saved my life at the risk of your own. I shall never forget that."

With that she was gone, the quick stride of her high-heeled boots receding down the Alto House corrridor.

From his bedroom window, Jim Hatfield saw her climb aboard Dall Stockton's waiting Conestoga, and the wagon headed off down the Thundergust Basin road.

Several hours still remained before sunset would bring Hatfield to another tour of duty as a hostler in Sam Rome's livery stable. Nevertheless he headed for the stable following his inverview with Beth Beloud, intent on getting his twin six-guns and shell-belts from Goldy's saddle-bag.

Entering the barn, he found the daytime hostler currying the magnificent sorrel in a back stall. He located his pegged saddle and unbuckled the *alforja* bags, unlocking them with a key which never left his possession.

It was dark in the straw-carpeted runway between the feed room and the mangers, and Hatfield worked unobserved as he swapped his rusty Colt .45, the one he had purchased here in Alto the morning before, for the handsome pair of matched Peacemakers which Buddy Ingalls had brought over from Presidio.

Sam Rome's stable office was separated from the spot where the Lone Wolf stood by a flimsy clapboard wall. Voices came from the office, and Hatfield cocked an ear as he recognized the guttural tones of the Blue Casino owner, Grote Postell.

"The Rafter B wrangler just pulled out from the mercantile with a load of supplies for the Beloud girl, Sam," Postell was saying to the stable boss.

"Know that," Rome grunted. "Sold young Stockton a set of hames and some chain tugs."

"There's a chance," Postell went on, "that Stockton or the girl may come back to town with the team later on today, and try to rent another wagon from yuh. Yuh're to refuse 'em, understand?"

There was a menacing note in Postell's voice, making his request seem like a flat order. Hatfield scowled, awaiting Sam Rome's answer.

"As yuh say, Postell," Rome grunted finally. "Reckon yuh're the kingpin around these diggin's."

Floor boards squeaked and a screen door slammed as Grote Postell made his exit. Peering through the archway of the stable, Hatfield saw the black-coated saloonman enter the Blue Casino across the street.

CHAPTER XI

Wagon Wreck

Puzzling over the information he had overheard, Jim Hatfield stepped out in front of the livery stable and paused to roll a cigarette. The office door opened and Sam Rome, wearing a troubled frown, came out on the steps. The deliveryman caught sight of the twin six-guns thonged low on his hostler's chap-clad legs and his brows arched curiously.

"For a drifter without a couple o' pesos to rattle in his pocket yesterday, you got yourself some right fancy hardware in a hurry, Field!" Rome commented suspiciously.

Hatfield fired his quirly and grinned.

"Won 'em at poker this mornin' with the last cartwheel from the wages yuh advanced me," he explained. "Any objections?"

The matter had already faded from Rome's brain, and his eyes had an off-focus look as his thoughts ranged far afield.

"By the way, Jim," the stable boss said abruptly, "a waddy from the Rafter B Ranch may drop in after yuh go on duty tonight, wanting to rent one of the extry wagons I got parked out behind the corral. Don't rent 'em or sell 'em any rollin' stock. Get that?"

Hatfield nodded. "You're the boss, Rome," he agreed.

A strange grin plucked at the corners of the oldster's mouth.

"Wish to blazes I *was* my own boss," he said enigmatically, and headed across the street, to vanish inside the Blue Casino.

A grim suspicion had been building up in Hatfield's head ever since he had eavesdropped on Postell's mysterious conversation with Rome. Dall Stockton and Beth Beloud had just left town, headed down the steep mountain grade which led to Thundergust Basin. Why was there a possibility that they would need another wagon to replace their heavily loaded Conestoga?

Unable to shake off a grim prescience that the Rafter B wagon was headed for trouble, Hatfield went back into the stable and accosted the daytime hostler.

"I could use a little fresh air," he commented to the man who was rubbing down Goldy. "Has the boss got any private stock that needs a little exercise?"

The hostler pointed toward a stall where a strawberry roan was pawing the floor of its stall.

"Big Red's gettin' too fat an' frisky," the hostler grunted. "Take him for a canter, if yuh want. Or cut yoreself any of the saddle stock out in the hind corral."

Hatfield threw a saddle on the roan, bridled it, and led it out onto the main street. From the hooked-back doors of the Blue Casino, he heard Postell's orchestra playing the music for Zolanda's "Hat Dance" number. He curbed an impulse to go into the gambling hall and see if the Red Duke was on hand to witness the entertainment which had embroiled him in a fist-fight with Hatfield yesterday.

Single-footing the frisky roan down between the rows of false-fronts, Hatfield did not give his borrowed mount its head until he struck the downgrade out of Alto.

Then, with the winelike mountain air beating against his face, the Ranger put the roan into a tight gallop, skidding around sharp hairpin curves as the Tombstone Trail stage road zigzagged its way down the Rosillos slopes in a series of switchbacks.

He passed occasional incoming riders, left them to breathe his dust. A mile below Alto the road straightened out for a mile, but he caught no glimpse of the Rafter B wagon ahead, nor did he see any telltale fumarole of alkali dust which should have marked the passage of the Conestoga.

The two-mile post flashed by before Jim Hatfield reined the fat strawberry down to a lope. He had made up his mind to ride as far as the basin flats, knowing he had to make the return trip in plenty of time to eat supper and relieve Rome's hostler.

Then, rounding a particularly sharp curve of the road, he came upon a scene of disaster.

Dall Stockton's heavily-loaded Conestoga had failed to make this hairpin turn, for some inexplicable reason. As Hatfield hammered down the slope, he saw the prairie schooner tipped over on its side, half off the road.

The sacked grain, reels of barbwire, and other purchases had spilled from the splintered box and the merchandise was scattered in disarray for a hundred yards down the cactus-dotted mountainside below the ledge road.

Reining up alongside the wagon, Hatfield's cheeks ballooned with relief as he saw Beth Beloud, dusty but apparently unhurt. She was talking to a rider on horseback some fifty yards from the scene of the accident.

Dall Stockton, his ruddy Irish face black with rage, was busy hitching his six-horse team to a juniper snag on the uphill side of the road. The harness had been damaged by the accident and on Stockton's left-cheek was a long, blood-smeared cut.

Swinging his gaze back to the wagon, Hatfield saw that it had lost a hind wheel. The missing wheel was in the bottom of the talus-littered ravine far below. The rear axle had snapped like a toothpick, and the wagon tongue had been reduced to kindling.

"What happened here, Stockton?" the Ranger demanded, swinging out of stirrups.

The Rafter B cavvy wrangler gave vent to a torrent of profanity, keeping his voice low so that his words would not carry to Beth, further down the road.

"Some skunk tampered with the hub-nut on my nigh wheel when I was back in town!" raged Stockton. "It took this far for the wheel to work off, on an outside curve. Danged lucky it didn't take me and Beth to our deaths down yonder."

Jim Hatfield pursed his lips thoughtfully, harking back to what Grote Postell had told his stable boss an hour ago: "The Rafter B may come back to town lookin' for a wagon to rent."

"Who'd play a dirty trick like that on yuh?" Hatfield demanded incredulously, already knowing the answer.

Stockton rubbed his cut cheek with a dusty knuckle.

"Some Coffin Thirteen rannihan out to make trouble for the Rafter B," the cavvy wrangler exploded without an instant's hesitation. "Postell's out to bust our outfit by hook or crook. This trick danged near put Beth out of the picture for keeps, too."

Hatfield watched Dall Stockton as the youthful cowhand inspected his team, hunting for possible injuries. Only a miracle had prevented the heavy Conestoga from rolling down the hill and dragging the fine draft horses to destruction.

Remounting, Hatfield rode down the road to where Beth was talking to a rider. The girl smiled shakily as she recognized the approaching Ranger. In the act of lifting his Stetson to greet Beth, Hatfield's eyes narrowed as he recognized the horseman with whom she was chatting—the Red Duke, mounted on the flaxen-tailed palomino which Hatfield had groomed last night.

"Mr.—er—Mr. Field, I want you to meet my fiancé, the Rafter B foreman," the girl said then. "Leon Hesterling, meet Jim Field. Leon, this is the gentleman who saved my life when the stage went into the river the other night."

Jim Hatfield could only stare. The Red Duke, then, was Leon Hesterling. Beth Beloud was engaged to marry a no-good drunken remittance man, the fop who had maltreated Zolanda Ruiz in the Blue Casino only twenty-four hours ago!

"It so happens," the Ranger said waspishly, "that I've had the pleasure of meetin' yore future husband, Miss Beloud. Haven't I, Duke?"

Leon Hesterling's too handsome face flushed crimson behind the blue-green bruises which Hatfield's clubbing fists had put there during their saloon brawl.

"Uh—I've met Field, darling," the Rafter B ramrod admitted. "He works in Sam Rome's stable. Took care of Palomar for me last night. Uh—I want to thank yuh for savin' my fiancée's life the other night, Field."

The Lone Wolf sat his saddle in grim silence, rubbing his scabbed knuckles. It was on the tip of his tongue to blurt out the story of Hesterling's shabby conduct involving a *bailerina,* but he curbed the impulse. After all, the Red Duke might have behaved as he did as a result of being in his cups. It was not Hatfield's affair, telling Beth Beloud a bit of gossip which would break her heart.

Beth laughed to bridge the awkward gap of silence which lay between the two men.

"You must excuse Leon's looks, Jim," she bantered. "He got in a fight with a drunk who tried to insult a dancehall girl at the Blue Casino yesterday."

Hatfield grinned at the ironic humor of this situation.

"Plumb fine of yuh, Hesterling!" he said pointedly. Then his manner changed as he turned to Beth. "Ma'am, I'll loan yuh this hoss so yuh can get back to yore home spread before dark. I'll go back to Alto with yore wrangler and see that he gets another wagon from Rome's yard. I'm sorry about this accident."

Beth's lips curled bleakly.

"Losing that wheel was no accident, Mr. Field," she said emphatically, twisting the diamond engagement ring which Leon Hesterling had given her. "Grote Postell was back of this so-called accident. I'm positive of that."

Hesterling regarded his future bride anxiously.

"Don't make that kind of *habla* in front of strangers, Beth!" he said earnestly. "Yuh have no whit of proof that the Coffin Thirteen tampered with that hub-nut. Rash talk will only lead us to trouble with Postell's bunch."

Beth gave the Red Duke a peculiar slantwise stare.

"Sometimes I think you're afraid of Postell, Leon!" she bit out. "Aren't we already up to our necks in trouble with the Coffin Thirteen? For once I'm inclined to agree with Dall."

Hatfield stepped out of saddle and turned the strawberry's reins over to the girl.

"Yuh can bring the bronc back to Rome's place next time yuh come to town, ma'am," he said. "I'll ride one of the wagon team back with Stockton."

Beth swung into stirrups with the lithe ease of a girl who had spent most of her adolescent years in the saddle, and favored him with a dazzling smile.

"I appreciate this kindness more than I can say, Mr. Field," she said. "Come on, Leon. Wing Sing will have supper waiting for us."

Hesterling flashed the Lone Wolf a last penetrating glance, reined about and rode after Beth. As the dust of their departure drifted back toward him, golden in the westering sunlight, Jim Hatfield walked back to where Dall Stockton was surveying the scattered freight which littered the mountainside.

"I work at Sam Rome's," Hatfield said. "He's got wagons to rent. I'll go back and help yuh mend that harness."

Stockton walked back to his waiting team and the two men scrambled astride the leaders. A few minutes later they were plodding back up the grade toward Alto.

"Stockton, I've got somethin' to tell you in confidence." Hatfield said after a lengthy silence between them. "I heard Grote Postell give my boss straight orders not to rent the Rafter B a wagon if yuh come back and wanted one."

The cavvy wrangler's eyes flashed wrathfully.

"Yuh see? That proves Grote knew an 'accident' was goin' to happen to that mudwagon of mine! By grab, I got a notion to go gunnin' for that range hog the minute I get back to town!"

Hatfield shook his head, noting that Stockton carried no guns, and was in no position to back up his threat.

"No, son. Listen. I go on duty at sundown. You meet me out behind the Tombstone Trail barn. I'll see that yuh get a wagon. If yuh can wait till mornin', I'll come down and help yuh load yore freight back on the relief wagon."

CHAPTER XII

"Field, Yuh're Fired!"

In silence, Hatfield and Dall Stockton covered another mile, Stockton's corrosive anger boiling inside him. More and more, Hatfield found himself drawn to the scrappy little wrangler. Contrasting him with the foppish Hesterling, the Ranger could not see how Beth Beloud had made the wrong choice between these two men who loved her.

"I'll tell yuh somethin' else, Dall," Hatfield said. "Just between the two of us. Hesterling didn't get his cut-up face fightin' for a girl's honor. I had the pleasure of workin' him over in the Blue Casino."

Dall Stockton regarded the man seated on the horse opposite him with a slow grin.

"So you're the ranny who cleaned that dude's plow for him!" Stockton said, reaching out impulsively to grip Hatfield's hand. "Mister, yuh're my friend for life. I'd give ten years of my misspent life to have punched the Red Duke myself!"

Seeing that Stockton was in a talkative mood now, Hatfield decided to feel him out.

"How come she wears Hesterling's ring?"

Stockton's face darkened with remembered grievances where his range boss was concerned.

"Hesterling come to the Rafter B when Beth was seventeen, four years ago. Charmed her with his city manners and his educated ways, for all he talks cowboy lingo. He's an English duke, yuh know. Has plenty of *dinero*. Old Cap'n Beloud sent her over to Austin to school. She got engaged to that rattlesnake last Christmas."

Hatfield gave the wrangler a long, level look.

"You love her yoreself, don't yuh?"

Stockton made a random gesture.

"Loved Beth since she was knee-high to the loadin'

gate of a Winchester, *amigo*. That's the trouble. I'm just a kid brother to Beth. Been kickin' around underfoot so long she can't see me for dust. That's why it rubs me so hard, seein' her throw her life away for a no-good tinhorn sport like the Duke."

The sun was settling into its appointed nest of fleecy clouds behind the Corazones peaks when they rode the team horses into the outskirts of Alto. They took a side way into town, and Stockton hitched the horses in a vacant lot behind the county courthouse. He accompanied Hatfield to the Alto House for supper.

Occupying the same table with them was the Ranger rookie from Presidio, young Buddy Ingalls. The two lawmen ignored each other. Shortly afterward, Ingalls went out to his waiting horse and headed westward, Presidio-bound, taking with him Hatfield's secret messages for relaying to Roaring Bill McDowell in Austin.

After carefully rehearsing future moves with Dall Stockton, Jim Hatfield headed for the livery stable. He ducked into the alley beside the Blue Casino and knocked on Zolanda Ruiz' door.

The Mexican girl was putting on her make-up for the evening show. In response to Hatfield's question, she informed him that she had seen no trace of Les Radley during the day.

"He must have lit a shuck for Mexico," Hatfield decided. "If he was goin' to show up around Alto, he'd be here by now. But keep a stirrup eye peeled for him, *querida mia*. If yuh locate him, I'll either be at Rome's barn or in Room F in the Alto House."

Zolanda squeezed his hand, hatred for Radley flashing in her black eyes.

"I hope he shows up," she said grimly. "I would like to burn candles over hees coffin, *es verdad*."

Leaving the alley, Hatfield crossed over to the livery stable, where the day hostler was fidgeting impatiently, waiting for his relief man to show up. Passing Rome's office, Hatfield saw the stable boss talking with Grote Postell and the county sheriff, Vic Drumm. By now, they probably had spotted Stockton's team.

An hour later, Jepp Vozar and half a dozen Coffin 13 riders galloped into town and left their mounts at Rome's place. Vozar tarried long enough to speak to Hatfield.

"The boss tells me yuh may be signin' up in my crew, Field," Vozar said. "Which will mean yuh'll draw yore wages from Grote and take yore orders from me. For that reason, I'm willin' to let that business of Freitas' killin' yesterday slide down the chutes. I got to be friends with men who work under me."

Hatfield eyed the *mestizo* foreman indifferently.

"Postell's jumpin' to conclusions, ain't he?" the Ranger said finally. "I told him I'd sleep on his offer. I ain't accepted it yet."

Vozar grinned contemptuously.

"When Postell makes a man an offer, he ain't generally turned down, Field. Rome pays yuh ten bucks a week, forty a month. Postell will pay ten times that much."

Hatfield nodded, saying nothing.

"Take a tip from a man who knows what he's talkin' about, Field," the Coffin 13 foreman went on. "Sheriff Vic Drumm has got yuh sized up as bein' on the dodge. If yuh ain't got a reward on yuh that Drumm can make yuh pay for, he'll back-shoot yuh just to show the voters he's on his toes. Think it over."

Vozar turned on his heel and disappeared in the direction of the Blue Casino, leaving Hatfield with a fresh problem to mull over. The chips were down. Postell had offered to rent his guns. To refuse that offer meant incurring Postell's enmity—which was tantamount to the Coffin 13 boss giving Sheriff Drumm the green signal toward putting him out of the way.

Any way Hatfield sized things up, his situation here in Alto was critical. There was even the possibility that Postell was entertaining suspicions that Rome's new hostler was perhaps a lawman in disguise.

"Might be a good idea to join the Coffin Thirteen crew, at that," Hatfield mused, and headed back toward the stable corrals to keep his appointment with Dall Stockton.

It was thoroughly dark now. As the courthouse clock chimed the hour of ten, Hatfield reached the vacant lot behind Rome's corrals where the stableman had a fleet of buckboards, buggies, and other wheeled equipment for rent or sale.

Dall Stockton was waiting with his six-horse team out in the chaparral behind the wagon yard. Within a few minutes they were hitching the Rafter B team to a big Studebaker freight wagon.

"Shore yuh can load that scattered freight by yoreself, Dall?" Hatfield asked, when Stockton was perched in the driver's seat, ready to roll. "I'd be glad to lend yuh a hand *mañana*."

"There'll be a moon up around midnight. I'll manage, Field. And thanks. If I can ever do you a favor—"

"Forget it, son. Try to get out of town without Postell or Sam Rome spottin' yuh."

The Rafter B wrangler vanished down a back street, keeping his team at a walk to muffle the rumble of the six-foot wheels on the Studebaker.

The rest of the night passed without incident. Promptly at dawn, Sam Rome appeared at the livery stable, accompanied by Jepp Vozar. The Coffin 13 foreman had spent the night in town, calling for his saddle horse only an hour ago.

"Field, I want to see you!" Rome sang out, anger shaking his voice. "Vozar says that Rafter B's freight ain't lyin' on the mountainside down below Hairpin Bend this mornin'."

Hatfield shrugged, meeting the hostile strike of Vozar's beady orbs.

"Why tell me about that?" he countered.

Vozar glowered angrily. "The Rafter B's only got one wagon big enough to haul that freight across the basin. That wagon's a wreck alongside the road. Dall Stockton had to get another wagon somewheres."

A crisis which Hatfield had anticipated had come sooner than he had expected. He turned wide, innocent eyes toward Sam Rome.

"Shore. I rented young Stockton one of yore spare

Studies last night, Sam. Five bucks a day until Rafter B returns it."

Rome's face turned livid. "Dang a man I can't trust!" he snarled. "Didn't I tell yuh not to rent any rollin' stock to Rafter B?"

Hatfield spread his palms. "Reckon I forgot yore orders, Sam. Besides, what's the diff? Yuh're in the wagon-rentin' game, ain't yuh?"

Vozar and Rome exchanged glances. Clearly, Postell's foreman was waiting for Rome to take action.

"I had reasons for not wantin' Rafter B to borry any of my wagons, Field. Yuh disobeyed my orders."

The Lone Wolf withered the old stable boss with his scorn.

"Yuh mean the Coffin Thirteen ordered yuh to help freeze out a small-tally spread, Rome. Why don't yuh have the nerve to come out with the truth?"

Rome groaned, avoiding his hostler's eyes.

"Field, yuh're fired! I paid you a week's wages in advance. Pick up and get!"

Hatfield's shoulders lifted and fell.

"*'Sta bueno* by me, Boss," he said contritely. "Reckon I'll have to look somewheres else for a job."

Rome stalked off into the barn, leaving Hatfield to face Vozar.

"You know how to get to the Coffin Thirteen, Field," Postell's foreman said. "I'll expect yuh at the bunk shack by noon. Only get this—when I give an order, yuh don't run a sandy on me. Not for five hundred smackers a month."

With which ultimatum Jepp Zozar turned and stalked off toward the Blue Casino.

Hatfield's gray-green eyes narrowed somberly. He was finished at Rome's livery, which meant he no longer had any valid excuse for remaining in Alto. But this no longer loomed important to the Ranger. He doubted more and more whether Les Radley would show up in this outlaw camp. The fugitive had probably crossed the Rio to seek sanctuary at the Mexican headquarters of the Tombstone Trail smuggler legion.

Going into the barn, Hatfield took his own saddle from its peg and proceeded to cinch it aboard Goldy. He was bridling the sorrel when Sam Rome emerged from the feed room.

"What yuh think yuh're doin'—saddlin' one of my customer's nags, Field?" Rome demanded.

The Lone Wolf finished buckling Goldy's headstall.

"Mebbe yuh better call the sheriff in to arrest a hoss thief, Sam," Hatfield suggested. "Because I aim to fork this sorrell."

Instead of betraying anger, the stable boss laughed.

"That nag is an outlaw, a one-man saddle bronc, Field. Belongs to an hombre who signed the book as B. Ingalls, from Marfa. I reckon he's the only man who can ride that geldin', because I tried straddlin' him yesterday and got throwed tail-over-tincup."

Hatfield smiled and led Goldy out to the street. Sam Rome did not realize the truth of his assertion. Goldy *was* a one-man horse, as he had demonstrated on more than one occasion in the past to the regret of would-be horse thieves.

"It just takes a good buckaroo to top him, Sam," Hatfield said, and swung into stirrups.

Goldy started bucking immediately—a common trait after a long period of inactivity—but the Ranger sat his saddle with consummate ease. The next moment Hatfield was heading down the street toward Thundergust Basin, with the golden sorrel as docile as a plow horse.

"Hey!" Rome shouted after him, running out of the stable. "I thought yuh was jokin', Field! Come back with that fuzztail!"

Twisting around in saddle, the Texas Ranger saw Rome making a beeline for Vic Drumm's jail—to report a stolen horse.

Swinging into a gallop, Hatfield put the town behind him. Half a mile down the road, he came upon Zolanda Ruiz, who made a habit of taking a long walk every morning. The Mexican girl flashed the Ranger a welcoming smile as he reined up beside her.

"Rome fired me this mornin', Zolanda," Hatfield reported. "From now on, scoutin' Alto for Les Radley will be yore job."

The girl's dusky eyes clouded.

"You are leavin' thees country?" she asked anxiously. "*Es bueno.*"

Hatfield shook his head. "I got me a cowpoke job lined up down in the basin, *querida.* I'll get to town ever so often."

Fear kindled in Zolanda's eyes. "You are a Coffin Thirteen *vaquero*, Senor Jeem?"

Hatfield picked up his reins.

"No," he answered. "I'm workin' for Beth Beloud on the Rafter B—if she'll have me."

CHAPTER XIII

Lavarock Canyon Assignment

Morning sunlight shafted through the window of the little office room in the Rafter B ranchhouse where old Captain Beloud had had his desk. Beth now occupied the martyred rancher's swivel chair, completing a detailed study of her father's books.

The Rafter B was definitely headed toward bankruptcy. Her father had died leaving considerable debts, including several months' back pay for his crew. Most of his riders had quit, following the old man's death.

Beef receipts for the last gather had been spent before the packeries had paid off, the Rafter B's income going to drovers' wages, railroad fees and current expenses. The supplies which Dall Stockton had brought down from the Alto mercantile house early this morning, in Sam Rome's rented Studebaker wagon, had not been paid for.

Within the next thirty days, Beth knew, Sheriff Vic Drumm would move in to tack up notices for a forced auction sale. And that would mean that Grote Postell would be the high bidder—probably the only one.

Rustlers had whittled at the Beloud herd until the last tally which Leon Hesterling had recorded in the books revealed that the Rafter B's stock totaled less than two hundred three-year-olds, yearlings and she-stuff. Even if Beth sold them at top market quotations, she realized that she could barely pay the wages of the three or four cowboys who had remained loyal to Rafter B.

She squared her shoulders and returned the books to her father's battered safe. Rolling down the top of the ancient desk, she made her way into the living room, where Leon Hesterling was seated on a horsehide divan, poking the logs in the fireplace.

Her foreman-fiancé looked up as she went to a front window and looked out over the Rafter B barns and corrals. Down by the granary, Dall Stockton, her wrangler, was unloading the Studebaker wagon, in spite of the fact that he had not slept all night. The redhead's industry filled Beth with a tender sentiment she was at a loss to analyze.

"Well, Beth"—Leon Hesterling spoke up now in his clipped British accents—"you jolly well know the answers after a look at Cap'n Bob's accounts. We're busted. Finished. For the last time, I'm advising you to accept the Coffin Thirteen's fifty-thousand-dollar offer."

Beth wheeled to face her fiancé, her face twitching angrily.

"No!" she cried, stamping her foot. "I'd burn the ranch down before I'd let Grote Postell get his hooks on Dad's place! If you don't want to fight that range hog, I do."

Hesterling shrugged, giving her a toothy smile which, on occasions such as this, she found maddening.

"Fight? With what? The Rafter B is helpless. You know it."

Beth shook her head, misery welling up in her. Just when she needed Hesterling most, he was failing her.

She knew little of his background—too little, she realized now, if she intended to marry the man. She realized vaguely that he was a scion of a wealthy Cornishman, in line for a dukedom, that his aristocratic family had shipped him off to Canada, where he had picked up his knowledge of cattle ranching before coming to West Texas and accepting the foremanship of the Rafter B.

"I wish you had more of Dall Stockton's gumption, Leon," she said desperately. "You should be out there this morning, helping him unload that barbed wire. If we are going to keep the Coffin Thirteen beef off our graze, we've got to string a drift fence, and soon."

Hesterling colored angrily.

"Maybe you should marry that cavvy wrangler, Beth!" he snapped peevishly. "Don't deny that he's tried to make love to you. I've seen the way he makes calf-eyes at you."

Beth crossed the room, planting her feet wide-spread in front of the remittance man.

"The Rafter B will be yours when we are man and wife," she reminded him. "I know you get monthly remittances from England, but why don't you help me save this ranch?"

Hesterling grinned indolently.

"And spend the rest of my life fighting the Tombstone Trail smugglers, to say nothing of bucking Grote Postell's combine? No, chickadee. If that is what being your husband entails, I don't want any part of it."

They were harsh words, intended to cut her to the quick, to break her iron resolution. Instead, they gave Beth an insight into this man's character. As if scales had been ripped off her eyes, she saw him now stripped of the aura of drama and swashbuckling romance which had made him appeal to her.

She saw him as he was, the product of a decadent nobility, a weakling who had no fight in his make-up, a quitter who chose the line of least resistance when the going got rough. In that moment, she made her decision, fully aware of its implications to her own future.

"Leon, you and I were not meant to be one. As a foreman, I respect you. As a prospective husband, I—I see my mistake."

Hesterling went bone white as he saw the girl jerk

her two-carat solitaire from her finger and thrust it into his hand.

"I want you to leave Rafter B, Leon," the girl went on, in a cold, impassionate voice. "Get out. I'll stay and fight this thing alone. I don't expect to win. But at least I'll go down without showing a yellow streak or a white flag."

Hesterling stared at the diamond ring in his hand, and then, with a cold laugh, he clapped on his Stetson and headed for the front door, his spurs chiming.

Hand on the knob, he turned to survey the girl.

"You're upset, chickadee," he drawled. "I'll go out and help your pet unload the wagon. By the time you've cooled off, I think you'll be glad to get my diamond back."

Hesterling stepped out on the front porch and paused there a moment, his lips clamped in rage, staring at the spears of dazzling light which flashed from the facets of the gem in his hand.

"Domestic trouble catch up with yuh, Red Duke?"

Hesterling looked up, startled by the deep bass voice which addressed him. He saw the man he knew as Jim Field sitting on a magnificent golden sorrel, a few feet from the porch steps.

There was a calculating grin on the Ranger's mouth as he saw Hesterling thrust the diamond engagement ring into a pocket. Before the ex-foreman of the Rafter B could frame a retort, Beth Beloud stepped out of the door beside Hesterling, her eyes shining as she recognized the rider.

"Howdy, ma'am," Hatfield drawled, doffing his Stetson. "Yuh offered me a job yesterday. If it's still open, I'm here to take it—on yore terms."

Leon Hesterling shook himself out of his trance.

"I do the hiring around this spread!" he snapped. "You can jolly well go to blazes, Field. I'll have no drifter working on the Rafter B."

Beth stepped to the edge of the porch, her amber eyes fixed on the Lone Wolf.

"Take your bedroll over to the bunkhouse," she

said evenly. "I'm hiring you—and I'm desperately glad to do so."

Hatfield replaced his John B., curveted Goldy around and rode off in the direction of the Rafter B bunk shack, with Hesterling staring after him like a man recovering from a body blow.

Hesterling turned to Beth then, his eyes humble, his manner contrite.

"Now, Beth, don't go off half-cocked," he pleaded. "You need a foreman around this place. I'm game to stick until the ship sinks under us."

Beth was staring off across the corrals to where Dall Stockton was laboring alongside the granary.

"No, Leon," she said, a deep sadness in her voice. "You and I are finished. I see that now. Believe me, this is not an easy decision for me to make."

Beads of sweat broke out on Hesterling's face and something akin to desperation showed in his close-set eyes.

"One last favor," the Rafter B owner went on. "Send Dall over to the house on your way out, Leon. I'm going to reward Dad's adopted son for his loyalty and devotion to this ranch. I'm going to make Dall Stockton my foreman."

Hesterling clenched and unclenched his fists. Then, without a word, he descended the porch steps and headed off toward the barns. He heard the ranchhouse door close as Beth went inside.

Instead of seeking out Dall Stockton, Leon Hesterling went directly to the Rafter B bunkhouse. Inside, he found Jim Hatfield spreading his blanket roll on an empty bunk.

"As long as Beth's hired yuh over my better judgment, Field," Hesterling said from the bunkhouse door, and reverting to range lingo, "yuh'll have to remember that I'm ramrod around this outfit. I've got a job for yuh to start off with this mornin'."

Hatfield hung his saddle-bags on a deerhorn rack over his bunk and turned to face the Red Duke.

"Fair enough," he rejoined. "What are yore orders?"

Hesterling stepped over to a table, brushed aside a beer bottle with a candle stub in its neck, a greasy deck of playing cards, and picked up a writing tablet. Taking a gold pencil from his vest pocket, Hesterling sat down and scribbled something on the tablet.

"What cattle we've got left," Hesterling said, "are bunched over in Lavarock Canyon. We've got a line camp over there with two waddies on duty—a buckaroo named Jinglebob Marsh and a Mexican *pelado* named Pancho. I want yuh to relieve 'em till further word from Beth or me."

Hatfield accepted the folded paper which the Duke handed him, and thrust it in the pocket of his hickory shirt. His pulses raced with quickening excitement.

Lavarock Canyon, he knew, was a link of the Tombstone Trail smuggling route. Part of the Rafter B range, it connected with the Rio Grande. He welcomed this opportunity to scout the critical Texas side of the beginning of the Tombstone Trail. "Hand my message to Jinglebob or the Mexican, over at our line camp cabin at the mouth of Lavarock Canyon," Hesterling went on. "Yoh'll find plenty of grub on hand. A week or ten days from now I'll send one of the men over to handle the herd in yore place. Until then, stick on the job."

CHAPTER XIV

Treachery

With his soogans rolled and cased in the slicker he carried behind his cantle, Jim Hatfield left the Rafter B bunkhouse and went out to where he had left Goldy drinking at a horse trough.

The Ranger was in rare good spirits. He was shrewd enough to know that he had witnessed the aftermath of a great crisis in the love affair of Beth Beloud and Leon Hesterling. Somehow or other, the girl had got wise to the fact that her financé was a rotter. Hatfield had been careful to note that her engagement ring was missing from her left hand, which meant that the ring Hesterling had been looking at was the symbol of a broken betrothal.

He saw nothing unusual in the fact that Hesterling remained at the Rafter B as its foreman. The Duke's role on the ranch was separate and distinct from his personal relationship with Beloud's heiress.

Within five minutes of his arrival on the Rafter B, the Lone Wolf had a job and his first assignment. Unwittingly, Hesterling had been instrumental in placing a Texas Ranger at the most crucial spot on the Tombstone Trail smuggling route.

Hatfield adjusted his cantle roll and mounted Goldy, aware that Hesterling was watching him through a bunkhouse window. He rode in the direction of the Corazone foothills, putting a shake-roofed blacksmith shop between him and the Red Duke's view.

A few yards away, young Dall Stockton, haggard-faced from his night of toil on the Alto road where he had lugged his scattered freight up the hill and loaded it on Rome's freight wagon, was finishing his work and unharnessing his team, preparatory to turning them out in the corral.

Stockton's fatigue-rutted face lighted up as he recognized the Ranger on the golden sorrel.

"Glad to see yuh, Field!" the cavvy wrangler called cheerily. "Fine hoss yuh're straddlin'. Never seen a finer bronc this side of the Pecos, and that's a fact."

Hatfield reined up, regarding Stockton benevolently.

"Dall, yuh told me yesterday that yuh was in love with Beth Beloud. Why don't yuh make a play for her, instead of backin' off into a corner stall and givin' Hesterling free rein?"

Stockton ran splayed fingers through his russet hair.

"Beth made her choice. Soon as they marry, I'm draggin' my picket pin. Yuh don't understand my position, Field."

The Ranger bent down from stirrups, his voice lowered confidentially:

"Beth gave the Duke his engagement ring back this mornin'. If I was you, son, I'd rattle my hocks over to the house and show Beth yuh're no man to be trifled with."

Stockton's jaw gaped in amazement, but a great hope dawned in his eyes as Jim Hatfield urged Goldy into a canter. The Ranger headed off past the barns, in the direction of the obsidian cliffs which marked the mouth of Lavarock Canyon, three miles to the west.

When Hatfield topped the first *tornillo*-spined hogback which put an embracing elbow of high ground around the Rafter B headquarters, he swung hipshot fashion in saddle and looked down on the roofs of the spread. He saw Dall Stockton walking rapidly toward the ranchhouse, and chuckled.

The cavvy wrangler had grown up with Beth, loved her like a sister. But it went deeper than that. Stockton, past twenty-one, was a man in love with a woman. The next time he saw Stockton, he hoped the wrangler would have some happy news for him.

The Lone Wolf was pushing off into the chaparral on his way to Lavarock Canyon when he saw a blur of movement off in the stunted cottonwoods which flanked the road from Alto. A rider was hammering into the Rafter B grounds, astride a cat-hammed buckskin cayuse.

Even at this distance, Hatfield had no difficulty in identifying the warped shoulders of the rider, the broad-brimmed black sombrero and the bannering tails of the clawhammer coat.

"Sheriff Vic Drumm" Hatfield chuckled, watching the bounty-hunting lawman from Alto gallop to a dusty halt in front of the Rafter B bunk shack. "An' I got an idea what he's after."

In the morning hush which overlay Thundergust Basin, sounds carried far. Hatfield waited on the trail, watching curiously, as he heard the unoiled hinges of the bunkhouse door squeak open and saw the tall figure of Leon Hesterling step out to greet the buzzard-faced sheriff.

"That Jim Field hombre stole a golden sorrel out of Sam Rome's livery this mornin', Duke!" Vic Drumm panted, his voice wafting up to where Hatfield sat his sorrel on the hogback. "I trailed him across the basin. He was headin' towards the Rafter B."

Hesterling's reply was voiced so low that the Ranger could not catch it. But Hatfield knew that Hesterling would like nothing better than to sick the law onto the man who had whipped him to a finish at the Blue Casino day before yesterday.

The Rafter B ramrod, however, instead of gesturing in the direction of Lavarock Canyon, motioned Vic Drumm to alight. Both men, heads close together in conspiratorial fashion, vanished inside the bunkhouse.

"Can't figger that," the Ranger grunted, touching Goldy's flanks with his rowels. "I'd of thought the Duke would have set that star-totin' reward-hunter on my trail *pronto prontico*. Especially seeing as how he didn't want to hire me in the first place."

Putting Goldy into a jogging lope, the Ranger fished in his pocket for makings and in so doing, encountered the note which Hesterling had given him to deliver to the cowboys he was to relieve out in the Lavarock Canyon holding ground.

Impelled by idle curiosity. Hatfield unfolded the missive and read the Red Duke's scribbled message:

> Pancho: Take the bearer back to where Jinglebob Marsh is and leave him there, as relief line-rider.
> Hesterling

The note seemed innocent enough in its phrasing, but Hatfield found himself wondering why the Duke had bothered to write it. It would have been sufficient for Hatfield to deliver his instructions to the *pelado* line rider verbally.

Returning the note to his pocket, Hatfield turned his attention to sizing up the country where he would be spending the next week riding herd on the remnants of the Rafter B's rustler-whittled herd.

The Corazone Range lifted sharply from the basin

flats, a seemingly endless succession of *barrancas* and boulder-dotted badland ridges which ended at the incised divide, shimmering against the brassy Texas sky. The mountain *malpais* was broken only in one place, by the twisting, haze-filled gulf of Lavarock Canyon. Over the summit, Hatfield knew, was the deeper gorge of the Rio Grande, setting off the Lone Star State from Old Mexico.

For half a thousand years, the trail of the Spanish *conquistadores* had occupied the pit of Lavarock Canyon. More than once, in conferences back in Austin headquarters with Captain Bill McDowell, the Lone Wolf had pored over survey maps of Lavarock Canyon.

Only a year ago, one of the McDowell's company of Rangers had been dispatched to ride patrol in this canyon, and that Ranger had never returned. As a result of his disappearance, McDowell had cooperated with the Mexican *Rurale* Police and the United States Border Patrol and Customs officials in keeping a watch on the point where Lavarock Canyon intersected the Rio Grande gorge.

It was at the junction of the Tombstone Trail with the international boundary line that one of the greatest smuggling leaks was located, McDowell figured. The results of the intensified campaign by Border authorities in both Texas and Mexico had been a temporary breakup of smuggling activities along the Tombstone Trail, and Les Radley's decision to hide out in the Rosillos sheep camp at Paisano Pass.

But of late, pressure of other duties had forced the governments of both nations to withdraw their guard from the local area. As a result, Jim Hatfield knew that he stood a good chance of spotting some *contrabandista* activity here in Lavarock Canyon. It had taken a strange and complex tangle of events to place him here, ostensibly as a Rafter B line rider. But instinct told the Lone Wolf that this assignment of Leon Hesterling's would not be devoid of its share of adventure and action.

Back in Presidio two weeks before, when Bill Mc-

Dowell's telegraphic orders had reached Jim Hatfield, the Ranger chief had hammered home his point. The telegram had read:

> LES RADLEY IS KNOWN TO BE HIDING OUT AT A PASTOR'S CAMP IN PAISANO PASS. BRING HIM BACK—ALIVE, IF POSSIBLE. RADLEY IS JUST A COG IN A BIG SMUGGLER ORGANIZATION. HE IS A DANGEROUS MAN, A RARE PRIZE. BUT WE ARE AFTER THE KINGPIN WHO GIVES RADLEY AND THE TOMBSTONE TRAIL BUNCH ORDERS. WITH RADLEY IN OUR HANDS, WE STAND CHANCE OF FINDING OUT WHO THAT LEADER IS.

Well, Hatfield had invaded Radley's hideout and had brought his man back to civilization—only to lose him. The only way Hatfield knew to restore his standing with Roaring Bill was to make his stay in the Thundergust Basin area count, and count big.

Thirty minutes out of the Rafter B, Hatfield reined Goldy to a halt on the rocky shoulder of Lavarock Canyon. Behind him, he could see the purple flats of Thundergust Basin, dotted with Grote Postell's grazing cattle. Sunlight flashed on the windowpanes of Alto town, midway up the Rosillos slopes, ten miles away.

A feather of dust lifted above the foothill ridges which Hatfield had just traveled. The Ranger's brows drew together in a quick frown as he caught a glimpse of Leon Hesterling and Sheriff Vic Drumm riding along his trail.

Drumm intended to arrest him for stealing Goldy from Sam Rome's stable. That would be an awkward charge to to buck, but at the moment of leaving Alto, Hatfield had seen no other way to handle the recovery of his own mount.

Dismissing his pursuers from his thoughts for the time being, Hatfield reined his sorrel down a ledge trail into the canyon proper. As far as he could see up into the cliff-hemmed gulch, there was no sign of Rafter B cattle or of grass where they could have grazed. Apparently Beth Beloud's stock were grazing further back in the mountains, closer to the Rio Grande.

Just inside the mouth of the canyon, where the gray ribbon marking the Tombstone Trail came in from the Thundergust Basin, Hatfield saw a low adobe shack. That would be the Rafter B line camp.

He rode up, sending his halloo running ahead of him, and dismounted, leaving Goldy ground-tied in front of the shack.

In response to his call, a seedy-looking Mexican peon in a straw hat and filthy serape emerged from the adobe *jacal*, a Remington .45-70 cradled in his arms.

"*Como 'sta?*" the Ranger greeted the Mexican. "You Pancho?"

The *vaquero* nodded, his flint-black eyes expressionless, his face an inscrutable mask.

"I'm here to relieve you and Jinglebob Marsh," Hatfield went on, speaking in Spanish. "Here's a *carta* from Senor Hesterling."

Pancho took the folded sheet of paper and scanned it stolidly.

"*Bueno*," he grunted. "Put bedroll inside. I take you up-canyon to Marsh."

Hatfield untied his soogans from Goldy's cantle and headed past Pancho into the murky interior of the cabin. And even as he moved Pancho drove the walnut butt of his rifle in a clubbing blow to the Ranger's skull.

Fireworks exploded in Hatfield's brain. He was not conscious of sprawling headlong across the threshold nor of the Mexican's deft fingers relieving him of his holstered six-guns.

CHAPTER XV

Jim Hatfield's Grave

Sheriff Vic Drumm and Leon Hesterling, riding into Lavarock Canyon by way of the rimrock trail which Jim Hatfield had followed, arrived at the Rafter B line camp. They found the Mexican, Pancho, busy tying the unconscious form of Beth Beloud's new cowhand in jackknife fashion across the saddle of the golden sorrel.

"That's the hoss he stole," the Alto sheriff announced triumphantly. "I'll take Jim Field back to my calaboose an'—"

Hesterling waved the lawman into silence.

"No. Stealin' a horse is nothing. I want my revenge, Vic. This waddy dies. Pancho will take him up the gulch and give him the same medicine Jinglebob Marsh got."

The two men dismounted, Vic Drumm scowling impatiently.

"As you say, Duke," the star-toter grunted. "Rome ought to be satisfied when I fetch his hoss back with blood on the hull. Jim Field's death is no skin off'n my nose."

Hesterling walked over to where Pancho was leading his own saddle horse away from the lean-to stable.

"Yore *hermanos* are coming through today?" the ex-Rafter B foreman asked the peon.

"*Si*, senor. The Rio ford, eet ees not guarded thees week. Then *mulas* loaded weeth *contrabando* are coming through from Tinaja Burro today."

Hesterling grinned with satisfaction.

"Good. Bring Field's *caballo* back with yuh after yu've buried the gringo, Pancho. The sheriff wants to take the sorrel back to town tonight."

Pancho slipped a rope over Goldy's head and set off up the cliff-bordered length of Tombstone Trail, leading the sorrel and its limp burden.

Hesterling walked back to where Vic Drumm was hauling a rawhide trot-line out of the cold springs which bubbled out of the rocks near the cabin. A series of beer bottles were tied to knots in the trot-line and shortly the two riders were refreshing themselves with ice-cold lager.

"We'll wait here," Hesterling said. "A ten-mule shipment of narcotics and bar silver is comin' up from Chihuahua. Pancho says the trail is open again."

Drumm wiped foam from his mustache and sought the shade of the cabin wall.

"Tough, you gettin' booted off Rafter B here at the pay-off," the sheriff commented. "Not that yuh're worryin' about losin' a wife, what with yuh havin' a missus back in England. But it would have been nice, ramroddin' Rafter B in yore own right."

Hesterling shrugged. "Don't matter much. Yuh'll be auctionin' off the spread to Grote Postell before the summer's over. I've still got plans of my own. . . ."

Jim Hatfield's senses returned slowly. He finally became aware of the fact that he was tied hand and foot, and that he was jackknifed over his own saddle. Goldy turned his head back frequently, whinnying sympathy.

Stinging alkali dust choked the Lone Wolf. Twisting his head around, he caught sight of a serape-clad figure mounted on a lineback dun which bore a Coffin 13 brand on its rump. The rider was Pancho, the horse was Grote Postell's. Those two facts were enough to snap Hatfield's dazed senses back to normal.

As his senses cleared, the Ranger realized that Leon Hesterling had deliberately sent him to a death-trap. Grote Postell had planted one of his Coffin 13 gunhawks at Beth Beloud's line camp. Hatfield found himself wondering if the other waddy, "Jinglebob" Marsh, was likewise drawing Coffin 13 pay.

After an interminable ride between towering volcanic walls, Pancho halted his dun and dismounted. Coming back to Goldy, the Mexican untied the *mecarte* which held his prisoner in saddle.

Hatfield sprawled heavily to the ground, landing on

his side. His skull ached like a shell of hot metal from the blow Pancho had given him with the rifle butt, and his brains felt as if they were being poached.

Drawing a twelve-inch *cuchillo* from his belt sheath, Pancho slashed Hatfield's ankle and wrist bonds, then hauled the Ranger to his feet. Stepping back, Pancho picked up his .45-70 and motioned Hatfield toward the mouth of a rocky defile which opened on Lavarock Canyon.

"Go that way, senor," the *pelado* ordered, speaking in guttural Spanish. "Follow my orders or I shoot."

Hatfield headed past Goldy, wondering in that moment if he would ever see the sorrel again. Catclaw and *ignota* scrub tore at his batwing chaps as he pushed his way up the boulder-littered defile, Pancho stalking behind him with his Remington at full cock.

Fifty yards from the Lavarock Canyon bottom, Hatfield came to a halt in a wide spot of the defile, floored with sand.

Directly ahead of him were two oblong mounds of earth, grown over with bull-tongue cactus. One of the mounds still showed the marks of the shovel that had shaped it.

They were graves, carefully hidden back in this deep cleft in the rocks. Topping the older of the two mounds was a silver star enclosed by a silver ring. A Texas Ranger's badge! On the newer grave were a pair of jinglebob spurs.

"Jinglebob Marsh," Pancho spoke up, reaming his rifle barrel against Hatfield's spine. "A Rafter B *vaquero* who was unlucky enough to see a band of alien Chinese being smuggled across the Border into Lavarock Canyon, *amigo*."

Hatfield stared, dumfounded by this evidence of ruthless killing, by Pancho's implied confession that he was a member of the Tombstone Trail smuggler legion.

"And the other?"

Pancho laughed harshly. "A Texas *Rangero*, who had the same bad luck, senor."

Hatfield bowed his head. This was where Captain Bill

McDowell's man had played out his string, then—bushwhacked while on patrol duty, by *contrabandistas* from south of the Border.

Pancho stepped over behind a clump of Spanish bayonets and brought out a rusty shovel.

"Dig, senor!" the Mexican ordered, handing Hatfield the tool. "A nice little graveyard we have here, no? But they call it the Tombstone Trail, it is so."

Hatfield stepped over between the two mounds and began digging. This was his own grave Pancho was forcing him to excavate at gun's point. Perhaps Jinglebob Marsh and the Ranger had known this same fate.

Under the loose sand, Hatfield's shovel stuck alkali hard pan, and digging was difficult. The nooning sun poured its punishing heat into the defile; the Ranger's shirt was soon drenched with perspiration.

Pancho crouched on a gabbro boulder near the rim of the Boot Hill clearing, keeping his rifle leveled at the Lone Wolf, taking no chances on his victim atempting a break.

Hatfield knew he was hopelessly trapped. Since Hesterling was the author of his downfall, he knew he could not count on the arrival of the Rafter B ramrod and the Alto sheriff for help.

By the end of an hour, he had gouged a three-by-six-foot oblong between the two graves, to the depth of a foot. As he worked, he groped desperately for some means of outwitting the rifle-toting Mexican who was supervising the grave-digging from behind a .45-70 muzzle.

Pancho was not to be bribed or tricked, Hatfield knew. The Mexican had his orders. He was a killer who was probably well paid for his rôle of executioner.

"Yuh work for the Coffin Thirteen?" Hatfield asked the black-faced peon, pausing in his work to lean heavily on his shovel.

"Keep digging," Pancho growled. "I make no *habla*."

Pancho was riding one of Postell's horses. That fact alone gave Hatfield reason to believe that the owner of the Blue Casino and the Coffin 13 Ranch had definite connections with the Tombstone Trail smuggling activities. But what good would that information do him now? Escape from this predicament was impossible.

His muscles cried out for rest, but Pancho would permit no stopping of his grim task. When the grave was a foot deeper, Hatfield was positive that Pancho would pull the trigger and drop his victim in the grave of his own making.

Then Pancho would strip some macabre memento from Hatfield—his sombrero, perhaps, or his boots—to serve as a grave marker. Then he would fill the hole and the fate of Texas' most celebrated Ranger would remain forever a mystery, another grave on the thousand-mile-long cemetery known as the Tombstone Trail.

Hatfield decided that his only chance for a break would be to heave a shovelful of clods into Pancho's face and follow it up by hurling his shovel like a javelin, hoping to split open Pancho's skull with the blade.

It was a long chance, in view of the rifle leveled at his brisket. Not for an instant did Pancho take his eyes off his grave-digging victim. But the break must come soon.

"*Bastante*—enough digging, senor!" Pancho said suddenly, as if reading Hatfield's trend of thought. "The grave ees ready. I geev you five seconds to say our prayers, *amigo*."

Hatfield saw Pancho stand up, cuddling the Remington stock against his leathery cheek, the barrel aimed at his heart.

Gripping the hickory shovel handle, Hatfield lunged forward, standing knee-deep in the grave, and hurled the shovel with all his force at the standing Mexican.

Pancho held his fire, leaping nimbly to the side as the steel blade of the shovel missed his skull by inches. Hatfield had made his one desperate bid for survival, and had failed. He was now at the killer's mercy!

Pancho grinned, enjoying this by-play.

"For that, senor, I shoot you and bury you alive!"

snarled the Mexican, and lined his sights on Hatfield's stomach.

Bracing himself for the expected impact of a .45-70 slug drilling his abdomen, Hatfield winced as a gunshot exploded like cannon fire between the defile walls.

But it was not Pancho's rifle which spat flame and smoke in that instant.

The Remington dropped from the Mexican's lax grasp, and blood spurted from a bullet-hole which appeared as if by magic between his bushy brows. With a long exhalation, Pancho toppled dead alongside Jim Hatfield's grave.

The shot had come from somewhere behind the Texas Ranger, not from the direction of Lavarock Canyon.

Unable to believe his eyes and ears, Jim Hatfield whirled and leaped out of the grave from which he had been so miraculously spared, staring into the dense growth of mesquites and junipers which blocked off the defile above him.

He saw a rusty rifle barrel jutting from the thickets, smoke wisping from its bore. Then the chaparral parted, to reveal a gnomelike figure clad in a parfleche jacket and battered Stetson. A pair of twinkling blue eyes regarded Jim Hatfield, and a toothless grin was revealed above a snarled beard which fell to the gunman's waist.

"*Smoky Joe!*"

Hatfield gasped out the name, as he recognized the wizened little prospector whom he had saved from Primotivo Freitas' knife over in Alto three days ago.

"That's right, son!" chuckled the desert rat. He stepped out into the full blaze of sunlight and leaned on his rifle. "I got a minin' claim at the upper end of this gully. When I heard the noise of somebody diggin' down here, I figgered them Border-hoppers had tallied another man for a nameless grave, so I come down to do private investigatin'."

Reaction set in on the big Ranger then, making him want to laugh immoderately. He seized the prospector's hand and wrung it.

"Yuh shore evened up yore debt to me, old-timer!" the Lone Wolf said fervently. "I was within an ace of seein' what lay over the Big Hill."

Smoky Joe prodded the dead Pancho with a warped boot toe.

"We'll bury this killer in the grave you dug, when it comes the cool of the evenin'," Smoky Joe grunted. "Right now, you could use a slug of forty-rod whisky and a snack of bait up at my prospect camp, I reckon."

Hatfield glanced off down the defile.

"I've got a hoss back in the canyon, Joe," he said. "Wait here and I'll be back in a jiff. I could use some nourishment."

CHAPTER XVI

Chihuahuan Smugglers

Going back down the defile from which he had never expected to emerge alive, the Lone Wolf's whistle brought Goldy over to the mouth of the gully. The sorrel was still linked with Pancho's Coffin 13 dun by a hackamore.

Looped over Pancho's saddle-horn were Hatfield's gun-belts and holstered Peacemakers. He buckled them on, snugging the big Colts against his thighs. Then he slipped the lead rope off Goldy and turned the Mexican's pony loose. Somewhere off up the canyon he heard a rushing of waters, and realized that the Rio Grande ford lay just around the bend of Lavarock Canyon.

He led Goldy back into the defile and found Smoky Joe seated on Pancho's back, calmly puffing a corncob pipe. The doughty old prospector got to his feet, appropriating the *pelado's* .45-70 and led the way into the screening chaparral.

A hundred yards up the brushy split in the rocks, Hatfield arrived at his rescuer's mining claim. Smoky Joe had blasted a prospect hole into a ledge, following a gold vein into the country rock. He made his home in a high-roofed stope just inside the grotto's mouth.

In the dim light, Jim Hatfield saw the outlines of a rusty army field stove, a canvas cot, and powder boxes tiered neatly and serving as a table. Further up the gulch, Smoky Joe's jenny mule was resting in a lean-to stable roofed with woven maguay fibers. A wheelbarrow and mining tools littered the heap of leveled-off mine tailings in front of the cave.

"Ever bothered by smugglers crossin' the Rio?" the Ranger asked, as Smoky Joe opened a can of peaches, a can of beans, and got sowbelly sizzling in a skillet alongside a pot of coffee.

The long-bearded oldster chuckled, tucking his whiskers in his belt as he stoked the army stove with 'squite chunks.

"This camp is too well hid," he explained. "But I've seed plenty of dope and 'dobe dollars and Chinese and other contraband come into Texas by way of Lavarock Canyon. Sometimes by night, sometimes in broad daylight."

Hatfield unbuckled his chaps belt and opened a cunningly contrived secret pocket sewn into the leather there. From the compartment he drew a silver-ringed star badge.

"Texas Ranger, eh?" Smoky Joe said, without surprise.

"Jim Hatfield's the name," the Lone Wolf said, returning the Ranger badge to its hiding place. "I'm takin' yuh into my confidence, Joe, because any help yuh can give me will be appreciated by the State of Texas."

Smoky Joe set out a steaming meal for his guest.

"Well," he remarked, "I can't help yuh, much, Hatfield. I don't interfere with them Border-hoppers as long as they leave me alone. When a man gits past eighty, he don't want to tangle in no shootin' match with Tombstone Trail smugglers."

Wolfing down the welcome food—a banquet could not have been more tasty to Hatfield in that moment—the Ranger decided that Smoky Joe, while friendly to his crusade here, needed drawing out.

"Where do these smugglers go after crossin' the Rio Grande?" he asked.

Smoky Joe shrugged his bony shoulders.

"After they leave Lavarock Canyon, they head into Thundergust Basin, like they was makin' for Alto town. I'm afraid I ain't much help to yuh, Hatfield."

The Ranger grinned. "Yuh shore are. Tell me—have yuh ever seen any of the Texans who take delivery on contraband?"

"Nope. The Border-hoppers turn their stuff over to their *compañeros* somewheres else beside Lavarock Canyon. Sometimes they come back loaded with freight for Chihuahua. Crated rifles and ammunition for the Mexican *rebelistas*, such as that. Depends on the political situation south of the Rio."

Jim Hatfield was helping himself to another cup of coffee when his ears caught the sound of voices somewhere outside. He was instantly alert, hands on gun butts.

"Somebody's located that Mexican I killed down the gulch," Smoky Joe explained. "Voices carry up the gully like they was talkin' into a megaphone. That's why I heard yuh diggin' yore grave."

Motioning for the prospector to remain where he was, Hatfield palmed his guns and headed out of the cave, going down the brushy trail toward the outlaw cemetery down the gulch. Moving with infinite stealth, he reached the spot where Smoky Joe had crouched at the edge of the clearing to draw a bead on the *pelado* killer.

Leon Hesterling and Sheriff Vic Drumm were standing beside Pancho's corpse, their horses visible further down the defile.

"I told yuh that shot didn't sound like Pancho's forty-five-seventy!" the Red Duke panted. "Sheriff, I don't like the looks of this. Jim Field made his getaway, somehow or other. Must have caught Pancho nappin'."

The Alto sheriff hitched his stooped shoulders nervously.

"Got away on that hoss Rome sent me out to dab my twine on," he grumbled. "One thing for shore, if I catch sight of that sorrel or Jim Field anywheres in my county, I'll shoot first and ask questions afterwards."

Jim Hatfield eared back the knurled prongs of his six-guns, opening his mouth to snarl out an order for the two conspirators to throw their arms up. But the words never left his lips. Leon Hesterling's next comment kept him mute.

"Let's get out of here. The shipment's due across the Rio. That's more important than worryin' about that saddle tramp makin' his getaway."

Drumm and the remittance man mounted, ignoring Pancho's unburied body. When they had vanished in the direction of Lavarock Canyon, Jim Hatfield skirted the clearing and stalked in pursuit.

A rumble of Mexican voices reached his ears before he came in sight of the pit of Lavarock Canyon. Skulking forward through the brush, Hatfield halted at the mouth of the defile.

A half-dozen Mexicans in gaudy serapes and steeple-peaked sombreros were gathered around Hesterling and the sheriff, jabbering excitedly. In the background were ten mules, dripping wet from the hocks down, proof that they had but recently forded the Rio Grande.

Each mule was laden with a Mexican *albarda* pack-saddle. The contents of the pack-bags was unknown to the Ranger, but he was positive they contained illicit freight from Chihuahua, consigned to some unknown accomplice in Texas.

The mules were hitched tandem. The leader of the Mexican smuggler party turned the trail rope over to Hesterling, who remained astride his palomino saddler.

"*Vaya,*" the Rafter B ex-foreman instructed the Mexicans. "Go. Yuh'll get yore pay-off *dinero* from *El Jefe* later this week, at the usual time and place. *Sabe?*"

The Chihuahua smugglers, eager to be rid of their dangerous cargo, turned the mules over to Hesterling and made their way back down the canyon in the direction of the Rio Grande. Hesterling passed the lead rope to the sheriff, who dallied it around his saddle-horn.

"We'll work it this way, Vic," the Red Duke said. "You hold the string at the line camp corral till dark. I'll ride over to Alto and tell the boss the shipment's here. We'll join yuh at the warehouse later."

Vic Drumm ran a finger around his collar.

"Well, I don't know," he grumbled. "I didn't figger on teamin' up that close with you smugglin' hombres. My job's to keep the law from botherin' you fellers."

Hesterling snapped an oath, reining his palomino alongside Drumm's stirrups.

"Yuh'll do as I say, Sheriff. Yuh're in this business up to yore turkey neck, and yuh know it. Nobody'll molest yuh, leadin' a string of pack-mules across the basin."

Drumm's defiance wilted and he got the smugglers' mules started in the direction of the Rafter B line-camp cabin. Leon Hesterling spurred his palomino into a gallop and disappeared ahead of Drumm and the mules.

Jim Hatfield holstered his guns. He had had two Tombstone Trail smugglers under a cold drop, caught red-handed with evidence enough to send them to the penitentiary in Leavenworth for long stretches. But a premature appearance now would hamstring his chances of finding out where the headquarters of the Tombstone Trail gang was located, as well as the rest of the membership.

Hesterling was on his way to Alto to report to the "boss." Later, the Rafter B foreman and the Tombstone Trail's chief would join Sheriff Drumm and the contraband-laden mules at a rendezvous which Hesterling had described as "the warehouse."

Where would the warehouse be? In Alto, perhaps? Somewhere on Thundergust Basin range? Or beyond the Rosillo Mountains? The answer to that riddle was simple. By trailing Sheriff Vic Drumm and the pack-mules tonight, he would be led to the answer of a puzzle which had harassed the State of Texas for a decade.

Heading back up the defile toward Smoky Joe's mining claim, Hatfield pondered the many ramifications of the case which this coming night should see brought to a victorious climax.

"The warehouse where the smugglers store their contraband could even be on the Rafter B Ranch," he told himself. "Mebbe that's why Captain Bob Beloud was killed—because he discovered the Tombstone Trail headquarters on his own place. One thing, Beth will be plumb upset when she finds out how close she came to marryin' an outlaw."

He found Smoky Joe toiling with pick and shovel at the gold deposits in the rear end of his tunnel. The Ranger briefly told the result of his spying on the transaction between the Chihuahua Border-hoppers and the two Texans.

"I aim to follow them mules wherever the sheriff leads 'em, Joe," the Lone Wolf said, and grinned. "I imagine there'll be plenty of surprises for me at the end of that trail. Whatever the outcome, I'll see to it that you get the State's reward for the capture of the Tombstone Trail smuggler chief. . . ."

At that very moment, Zolanda Ruiz was taking a nap in her private quarters on the top floor of Grote Postell's Blue Casino gambling dive in Alto.

She had song and dance numbers to perform every two hours until daylight, for this was a Saturday night and Alto would be crowded with men avid for entertainment. Zolanda Ruiz was Postell's star performer, along with a bevy of can-can dancers. Those dancers spent all their time off-stage mingling with the Casino's customers, drinking watered wine while they enticed their patrons to buy expensive liquor from Postell's bar.

Postell paid these girls a percentage of their nightly take, as was the frontier custom, but Zolanda's talent as a songstress and dancer lifted her above this shabby level.

She was not required to mingle with the Blue Casino's customers unless she desired to do so.

Sleeping peacefully, the Mexican girl was not aware of the door of her room opening, to admit a tall, chunky-shouldered man. He wore a dirty linsey-woolsey shirt and butternut jeans stuffed into warped, mud-caked cowboots. His sombrero was a battered *sisal* straw affair which a Mexican peon would have scorned.

An inch growth of beard furred the man's plowshare jaw. His hands were dirty and his fingernails were black and broken. The only thing about the intruder which marked him as different from the saloon barflies were his guns—fine cedar-stocked Peacemakers in fancy-tooled oak-tanned leather holsters. The loops of the crisscrossed belts were filled with the brass and lead tips of .45 cartridges.

CHAPTER XVII

Peril in Alto

Closing the door softly behind him, the intruder into Zolanda Ruiz' room stared in rapt absorption at the curvesome woman in the scarlet-and-lemon dancing costume who lay curled on the bed, beside the open window. In repose her face was somehow unlovely, minus its rouge and lip paint and mascara. Her facial muscles were beginning to sag, and the streaks of gray were visible close to her scalp, where the hair had grown out after the rest had been dyed. She was snoring slightly, unglamorous in sleep.

"Washed-out hag," the man muttered digustedly.

Then he spotted a bottle of imported bourbon on Zolanda's bedside stand. He swigged deeply from the bottle, and smacked his lips. No cheap trade liquor, this. Zolanda must have tapped Grote Postell's private stock of Taos lightning. He corked the flask-shaped bottle and thrust it in a pocket of his jeans.

Going to Zolanda's dresser, he rummaged through drawers filled with filmy feminine clothing. A faint aroma of sachet cloyed his nostrils, rousing old memories and old hungers in the derelict.

In the bottom drawer he found what he was hunting for—a purse. He helped himself to the currency and silver *pesos* it contained, and grinned with satisfaction.

There was a hobnail lamp with a globular shade on

the washstand beside a bowl of water and a cracked pitcher. He lit the lampwick, then stepped over to the window, glancing down on Alto's main street which was drowsing in siesta.

Grote Postell and Leon Hesterling emerged from the gambling hall below him and stepped into the saddles of a pair of horses hitched to the Blue Casino's tierack. The Red Duke's palomino was dripping lather, evidence that Hesterling had recently come in off the range.

The prowler opened his mouth to call down to Postell, then thought better of it. He believed he knew Postell's destination. He watched the two riders canter off down the street, their horses' hoofs lifting spirals of yellow dust as they headed in the direction of Thundergust Basin. Then the man at Zolanda's window reached out and hauled down the green window blind.

The sudden darkening of the room, the contrast between the westering sunlight and the pale glow of the coal-oil lamp, caused Zolanda to stir and open her eyes.

Then she sat bolt upright, her dusky face going ash-white as she saw the brutish-faced man towering over her.

"Les!" she gasped, lifting a jeweled hand to her throat. "You—you've come back!"

Les Radley laughed harshly, reaching down to grip her by the arms and haul her to her feet.

"Ain't yuh got a kiss for yore husband, Zola?" he asked, the whisky odor on his breath striking her face.

Zolanda was full awake now, and rage and contempt washed the terror from her eyes as she wrenched free of him and stepped back, sinking into a Morris chair.

"I'm not your wife!" she panted huskily. "Not for ten years have you paid any attention to me. Why are you bothering me now?"

She spoke in Spanish, which the Tombstone Trail smuggler understood as well as he did his native tongue. Radley seated himself in a chair by the foot of the bed, drew a cigar from his shirt pocket, bit off the end, and lighted it over the hot chimney of the lamp.

"Four days ago," Radley said, "a Texas Ranger had

me hogtied for brandin'. A washed-out bridge over on the Tornillo wrecked the stage he was takin' me in to a hangrope. I've spent the last four days hidin' out at a friend's shack back in the hills, Zola."

The Mexican girl stared at this man who was her legal husband as if she were seeing a rattlesnake coiled to strike. Indeed, this outlaw was as dangerous as a sidewinder, and more so.

"I come to Alto," Radley went on, "to see Grote Postell. I missed him because I wanted to see you first, sweetheart. I just seen him and that Limey dude, Hesterling, headin' out for the Coffin Thirteen."

Zolanda sat rigid in her chair, wondering why Les Radley had bothered to look her up. The love they had once known was dead, she knew. For years she had known only hate for this man who had never shown her anything but cruelty.

It occurred to her that Radley had come here to kill her. She could not shake off the premonition. And she was unarmed. The only weapon she owned was a derringer which was in the drawer of her vanity table, downstairs in her dressing room.

"The Ranger who dabbed his loop on me over at Paisano Pass where I was holed up," Radley went on, "was yore old friend, Jim Hatfield. Used to be sweet on him over in Del Rio, remember? And he couldn't see yuh for dust."

Zolanda bit her lip, old pangs of heartbreak stirring her.

"These are Hatfield's guns I'm wearin'," Radley went on, puffing cigar smoke at the ceiling. "It's bad luck, I didn't get a chance to use 'em on the Lone Wolf. But I thought he drowned in the Tornillo. Seems I was mistaken, though."

Zolanda betrayed her alarm then by sitting up suddenly, a pulse hammering on her throat.

"Comin' into town this afternoon," Radley went on in his surly monotone, "I overheard some rannies talkin' about a jasper by the name of Jim Field, who stole a golden sorrel from Sam Rome's stable early this mornin'. Seems the sheriff's out lookin' for Field right now."

The Mexican girl closed her eyes to shield from the outlaw who sat across the room the terror which they held.

"Jim Hatfield owns a golden sorrel," Radley said, staring at her sharply. "I got a hunch this Jim Field was the Ranger I'm lookin' for. He managed to keep from drownin' and headed for the nearest settlement, which is Alto."

Radley came to his feet, crossed the room and seized Zolanda's shoulder in a viselike grip.

"If Hatfield's been stoppin' in Alto till today," he snarled viciously, "I know yuh've seen him. You two are friends. Which means yuh know where Hatfield's *vamosed* to."

Zolanda winced from the pain of his crushing grip.

"No—no!" she panted hysterically. "I—I haven't seen *El Lobo Solo!* I know nothing of this Senor Field!"

Radley's mallet-sized hands gripped her by the throat then, his thumbs questing for her windpipe. Shaking her as a terrier would shake a rat, Radley pulled her to her feet.

Then, holding her throat with his left hand, the outlaw pulled a bowie knife from a sheath inside his shirt and thrust the razor-honed blade against her scarlet dress, over the heart.

"Tell me where that Ranger is, Zola, or I'll carve yuh up like a chicken in a butcher shop!"

The sharp *cuchillo* penetrated Zolanda's dress, pricked the skin over her heart. A whit more pressure, and she would have six inches of cold steel in her lungs.

"Yes—yes!" she whimpered. "Senor Hatfield has—has been here. I saw him, talked to him."

Radley increased the pressure of his knife blade, twisting it a little, his left hand ready to strangle off any scream she might utter.

"Where's he gone?" he snarled in a steely whisper.

Zolanda felt faint. Her mind worked desperately,

seeking some avenue of retreat from this terrifying pre-predicament.

"Senor Field has gone to the Coffin Thirteen, Les," she panted. "Postell has hired him. You will find him at Postell's *rancho.*"

Radley sheathed his knife and, doubling his fists, smashed a short brutal blow at the woman's jaw, knocking her back into the chair. She sagged limply, and he saw that she was unconscious.

For a moment Radley stood staring at his estranged wife, sorely tempted to thrust his knife into her throat. Then, with a shrug, he went to the door and stepped out into the corridor.

Zolanda rallied to her senses in a short time. Groggy with fear and pain, she staggered to the window and ran up the shade, drawing some fresh air into her lungs.

Then she stiffened, as she saw Les Radley emerging from the Tombstone Trail Livery barn. Sam Rome was leading a saddle horse out of the stable, and she saw Radley hand the old man a greenback.

Swinging into saddle, the outlaw spurred his rented mount into a lope and headed down the street toward Thundergust Basin. He was on his way to Grote Postell's ranch, searching for the Texas Ranger he intended to kill in cold blood!

He would not find Jim Hatfield on the Coffin 13 but in all probability Radley would remain at Postell's place.

Wiping the blood from her bruised jaw, Zolanda Ruiz donned a Spanish mantilla and went downstairs into the Blue Casino. Going backstage, she paused in her dressing room long enough to get the .41 single-shot derringer from her vanity table drawer.

Then, leaving the establishment by the alley door, she crossed the street to Sam Rome's livery. Grote Postell was out of town, so he would not know of her failure to appear on the Blue Casino stage tonight.

Zolanda owned a leggy *grulla* mare, which she frequently rode for exercise. She saddled the *grulla,* without attracting the notice of either Sam Rome or his hostler.

Shortly she was riding down Alto's main street, grim and aloof in the saddle, oblivious to the waves and calls of men who knew her. She sat the saddle like an automaton, knowing that for her, life had played out its string, that she had a tryst with destiny this night. For she had made up her mind to track Les Radley to the Coffin 13 and kill him before he got a chance to bushwhack Jim Hatfield.

Her mare was fat and old and lazy, slow as a plow horse. She knew she had no chance of overtaking Radley on his way to the Postell spread. But she could bide her time to strike.

Ahead of her, the Tombstone Trail pointed like a chalkline across Thundergust Basin's cattle range, toward the remote cluster of buildings in a crease of the Corazone foothills which marked Beth Beloud's Rafter B Ranch.

Zolanda visualized Hatfield over there now, sitting in on a bushwhack game in which Beth was putting her feeble strength and resources against the might of Grote Postell. Thinking of that, Zolanda regretted that her derringer had but one bullet in it. As long as she had steeled herself to kill a man, putting herself in purgatory for all eternity, she might as well include Grote Postell. Texas would be better off without him, and his ambitions and his intrigues.

But the derringer was a single-shot weapon, and Les Radley's name was on the cartridge in that gun. Sundown would overtake her before she reached the Coffin 13, but darkness would be in her favor on this manhunt. . . .

An hour after sundown, when darkness pooled swiftly in indigo layers across the expanse of Thundergust Basin, Jim Hatfield saw Sheriff Vic Drumm emerge from the Rafter B line-camp cabin at the mouth of Lavarock Canyon. Throughout the afternoon, the Lone Wolf had watched from the south shoulder of the canyon entrance, bellied down like a lizard on a ledge of volcanic rock which gave him a view of the line camp below.

Drumm had driven the ten contraband-laden mules into the shelter of the lean-to behind the rock shack, out of sight of any passing rider who might chance by. Except for periodic trips to the trot-line beer bottles, submerged in the ice-water spring, the Alto sheriff kept indoors, out of the sweltering Texas heat.

Now, with darkness shielding his activities, Drumm saddled his horse and left the Rafter B camp, trailing the ten pack mules.

Their shape was a serpentine shadow under the stars.

Jim Hatfield waited for ten minutes before going back into a *chamiso*-tangled arroyo where Goldy was picketed. Saddling hastily, the Ranger rode down a long ledge which brought him to the basin floor.

He had no difficulty in picking up Vic Drumm's trail in the darkness, for the pungent odor of dust from the mules' passage lay in the humid air.

That gave Hatfield a blue-printed trail to follow.

CHAPTER XVIII

Smugglers' Den

Knowing that the sheriff had little stomach for this business of transporting smuggled goods along the Tombstone Trail, Hatfield knew Drumm would be on a hair-trigger edge. That would make him nervous enough to shoot at anything he saw or heard. So Jim Hatfield held Goldy to a singlefoot pace, though the big gelding was chafing at the bit, wanting a hard gallop to work off excess energy.

The Ranger was trailing Drumm by sound more than sight, keeping a good hundred yards behind the sheriff's cavalcade of mules. Every few minutes, the Texas Ranger reined up, keening the night with hands cupped behind ears. He could not afford to let Sheriff

Drumm give him the slip tonight. But always he picked up the thud of hoofs, the creak of *albarda* saddle pouches, the occasional trumpeting noise as one of the flop-eared mules blew dust from its muzzle.

Drumm skirted the hogback which cut the Rafter B buildings from view and swung off the Tombstone Trail wagon wheel ruts, skirting the ancient traveling route, ubut keeping a hundred yards out in the sagebrush.

When the lighted windows of Beth Beloud's place finally came in view, Hatfield estimated that he had trailed the mules three miles out into Thundergust Basin. There was a moon due later tonight, but its pale promise was not yet visible behind the jagged teeth of the Rosillos. Far to the east, the cluster of lights marking Alto town, halfway up the footslopes, twinkled like a cupful of diamonds against the ebon backdrop of the mountains.

Midway across the Basin floor, Vic Drumm turned abruptly north and crossed the Tombstone Trail. Jim Hatfield noted this change of direction with interest, for it seemed to indicate that Alto was not the sheriff's destination.

Would it be Grote Postell's Coffin 13, then, which lay in the Rosillos foothills north of the cowtown? But as the plodding mules put the miles behind them, Hatfield began to doubt this. Already, the lights of the Coffin 13 bunkhouse were behind them, and unless the sheriff turned another right angle, he was passing up Postell's ranch.

Gradually the sheriff swung back toward the Corazones, and finally struck a little-used wagon road which snaked back into the foothills north of the Beloud ranch. Hatfield closed up the gap to fifty yards from the rearmost mule now, knowing that the risk of losing trace of Vic Drumm was increasing sharply as the road led between low hills thinly timbered with loblolly pines.

They came to a fork in the wagon road, and there was enough star glow reflecting from the Texas sky to enable Jim Hatfield to read a name on a rusty R.F.D. mailbox there:

WINEGLASS RANCH
MICHAEL JACKSON, OWNER

The right-hand fork, Hatfield deduced, led down to the Rafter B, and Vic Drumm was taking the smugglers' mules up the Wineglass trail. Remembering something which Zolanda Ruiz had told him he recalled that Michael Jackson had been one of the homesteaders who had been frozen out by the onward march of Grote Postell's ever-expanding cattle kingdom.

An owl hoot sounded somewhere ahead, and the Lone Wolf reined Goldy up quickly as he heard another owl hoot answer—a clumsy imitation, this last, which came from Sheriff Vic Drumm.

Smugglers up ahead were signaling to the incoming train!

It was too risky for horseback approach, now. Hatfield swung out of stirrups and ground-hitched Goldy behind a *motte* of junipers and scrub aspen. Then, guns palmed, he headed up the road, keeping handy to the brush alongside the right-of-way.

Limned against a white alkali hillside, Hatfield saw the looming buildings of the Jackson homestead not fifty yards away. The chalky slope picked out the shapes of Vic Drumm and his ten tandem-hitched mules.

A chaps-clad man was striding toward the sheriff as Hatfield slipped along a broken-down corral fence on his hands and knees, getting closer to the men and alongside the pack-saddled mules.

"Took yuh long enough, Sheriff," a voice came through the shadows to Hatfield, a voice which was familiar, but which he could not place at the moment.

"I played it safe and circled wide of the Beloud ranch, just in case Dall Stockton was out scoutin'," the sheriff answered. "Beth made Stockton her foreman, the Duke told me."

Hatfield grinned at this news. So Beth had fired Leon

Hasterling! Which probably meant she had done that even before the Rafter B ramrod had dispatched Hatfield out to Lavarock Canyon, into Pancho's death trap this morning.

"Lead the mules into the warehouse, Vic," the guttural voice went on. "I'll help yuh unload."

"All right, Vozar," came Drumm's meager voice.

Vozar! Jepp Vozar, Grote Postell's *mestizo* foreman from the Coffin 13! Bits of the jigsaw puzzle were falling into place rapidly tonight. Postell's ramrod, at any rate, was a member of the Tombstone Trail rustler band!

Hatfield heard hinges creak as Jepp Vozar opened the doors of a long-walled barn—the "warehouse" where smuggled goods were stored, apparently. He saw Vic Drumm lead the mules into the building, saw Vozar close the door behind them.

Emerging from the brush, the Lone Wolf stalked across the open ground and paused alongside the barn. The air had a pungent, earthy smell here, the smell of arid ground recently soaked by the rainstorm earlier in the week.

Cicadas trilled in a nearby greasewood thicket. Off to the left, he heard horses stamping in the stalls in a barn. Apparently Jepp Vozar was not alone, here on the isolated Wineglass homestead.

Finding a chink in the logs where moss packing had fallen out, Hatfield squinted into the "warehouse." What he saw brought an under-breath oath to his lips.

Mike Jackson had built this structure for a granary, but it was used for a more nefarious purpose now. Jepp Vozar had lighted a lantern, and its pale beams glinted off tiers of silver ingots, off wall shelves lined with tin cans and small sacks. Hatfield had little doubt as to what those cans and sacks contained. Narcotics—heroin, morphine, opium, marijuana! He had found the depository of the Tombstone Trail smuggling band!

Jepp Vozar and the sheriff were busy unloading the mule-packs and storing them in a pile in one corner, almost outside the limited range of Jim Hatfield's vision. Vic Drumm was obviously laboring under a severe nervous strain tonight, for his vulturelike face was rinsed with cold sweat and his hands shook as he unsaddled the Mexican mules.

"The boss is over at the house," Jepp Vozar said. "There's a little pow-wow goin' over there that'll make your eyeballs bug out a foot, Sheriff."

Hatfield put his ear to the crack in the log wall to catch Vic Drumm's answer.

"No dice, Jepp," it came. "I'm lightin' a shuck back to Alto. I don't want no part in this smugglin' business."

The steely silence in which Jepp Vozar heard this disclosure made Jim Hatfield put his eye back to the crack in the wall. He saw Drumm tightening the latigo of his saddle. The Coffin 13 *segundo* was watching him angrily, hand on gun-butt.

"Runnin' out on the bunch, Sheriff?" the half-breed demanded acidly.

Sheriff Drumm shook his head.

"No—just goin' back where I belong. The boss gives me my cut to keep star-toters from breathin' down his neck. I'm satisfied to live off of what I get from owlhooters like Les Radley, and the owlhooters I can collect reward money on. Smugglin's too risky for me."

Hatfield saw Vic Drumm lead his horse over to the warehouse door and reach for the big wooden bar which closed it. Behind the sheriff, Jepp Vozar slipped a bowie knife from its sheath behind his shirt collar and hefted it, laying the haft along his brown palm.

"I think," Vozar said in a grating voice, "that yuh're turnin' yeller on us, Drumm."

Something in Vozar's tone warned the sheriff of danger behind his back, and he whirled, one bony hand going to his gun butt.

Hatfield gasped as he saw Vozar take one step forward, his arm blurring up and out. The Mexican knife lanced through space like the dissolving scratch of a shooting star across the night sky. Vic Drumm choked out an oath, his gun half out of holster, and stared down at the quivering hilt of the bowie knife which jutted from his ribs.

Then, with a gagging exhalation, the sheriff fell dead on the puncheon floor, his stooped shoulders quivering.

"Should have done that long before now," Vozar muttered, and blew out his lantern.

Jim Hatfield braced his back against the warehouse wall as he heard Vozar open the warehouse door. He remained standing there as the Coffin 13 foreman led the mules over to a corral and turned them loose there.

Then, a gray ghost in the starlight, Vozar headed around the corner of the warehouse. Hatfield slipped along the wall in catlike silence.

Fifty yards beyond the warehouse was the squat adobe ranchhouse which Mike Jackson had built when he had homesteaded the Wineglass. Cracks of light showed behind shuttered windows.

Inside that adobe, the chief of the Tombstone Trail gang—whoever he was—was engaged in some sort of sensational "pow-wow," according to what Vozar had told the sheriff. Vic Drumm had tried to avoid joining that pow-wow. But Jim Hatfield had exactly the opposite intention.

He was halfway to the Wineglass house when he saw Jepp Vozar open the door, silhouetted sharply against the lamplight within. Then the Coffin 13 foreman closed the door behind him.

The Lone Wolf stalked across the front yard and paused at that door. Muttered voices reached his ears as he moved the Texas Ranger star from his belt hideout and pinned it in plain view on his shirt. He jacked open his six-shooters and inspected the loaded chambers.

Showdown was just ahead, perhaps a gunsmoke showdown. When he opened that door, he had to be prepared for shoot-out. . . .

Earlier that evening, Dall Stockton left the Rafter B bunkhouse and entered Beth Beloud's living room. He found the girl helping their Chinese cook, Wing Sing, prepare supper. The redhead who was Rafter B's new foreman, as of noon today, had a worried look on his face.

"Funny thing, Beth," he said, "but I can't find hide

nor hair of that new waddy, Jim Field. He didn't leave his soogans at the bunkhouse, and his sorrel ain't in the cavvy corral."

Beth shook her head, puzzled. All afternoon she had been wondering what had become of the man she believed to be Les Radley, the wanted outlaw.

"Yuh know, after yuh give Hesterling his walkin' papers this mornin', he rode out with Sheriff Drumm," Dall Stockton went on. "Yuh suppose they had anything to do with Field's *vamosin'?* I happen to know that Field and Leon were enemies."

Beth gave her foreman a long, searching look. He was in love with her, she knew, and could be trusted with her secret.

"Dall," she said softly, "I have a confession to make. Jim Field isn't his real name. He's a wanted outlaw who recently escaped from a Texas Ranger—the night he saved my life when the stagecoach went into the Tornillo. His real name is Les Radley."

Stockton's jaw sagged in amazement.

"Radley! The deuce yuh say! But—but why hire a killer lobo like Les Radley? You and yore father always used to say—"

"If we're going to fight Coffin Thirteen," she cut in swiftly, "we've got to have gunmen to back us, Dall. You know and I know that Radley is a good man in some ways, despite his killer rep. We—"

A knock on the door made the girl break off. Catching her signal, Dall Stockton answered it.

Jepp Vozar stood at the threshold, an envelope in his hand.

CHAPTER XIX

Death Trap

Unheeding Dall Stockton's angry frown—Dall and Vozar were enemies of long standing, and Stockton had warned the Coffin 13 breed never to set foot on Rafter B soil—Vozar stepped into the room and handed the envelope to Beth Beloud.

"Leon Hesterling is in trouble, ma'am," Vozar said. "It's up to you to help him out of it."

Scowling, Beth tore open the envelope and scanned a letter written in Leon Hesterling's handwriting:

> Beth, sweetheart:
>
> After you returned my ring today, I know I have no right to ask you for favors. But I am being held a prisoner at Mike Jackson's old homestead. You have it in your power to save my life. I can't explain until I see you. If you have any mercy, accompany Jepp Vozar to the Wineglass. I promise you no harm will come to you. It means life or death to me.
>
> Leon H.

She handed the letter to Dall Stockton, who read it swiftly.

"Hesterling's hide ain't worth savin'," he bit out. "Tell Vozar to go to blazes, Beth, before I throw a gun on the breed."

Vozar shrugged and turned toward the door.

"No—I'll go!" Beth cried after him. "Dall, it's the least I can do, if Leon is really in danger. This note is no forgery."

Stockton clamped his jaw grimly, then strode over to a gun rack and took down a Winchester deer rifle.

"I'm comin' along," he insisted. "I wouldn't let yuh

ride anywhere alone with Jepp Vozar for a million dollars."

From the kitchen doorway, the wizened old Oriental cook piped up in his nasal sing-song:

"Wing Sing go too, Missy Beth."

Five minutes later, Jepp Vozar was leading the three Rafter B riders up the wagon road which skirted the Corazone foothills. The Chinese had armed himself with two hatchets.

It was a half-hour ride to the Wineglass. They reached Mike Jackson's RFD mail-box at the road fork and turned left, and only Vozar caught sight of Sheriff Vic Drumm and his mule string, approaching the works from the east.

Reaching Jackson's adobe, the riders dismounted and climbed the porch steps, Stockton and Wing Sing bracketing the girl. The door opened and Grote Postell stepped out to meet them, twin six-guns jutting from his fists. Their bores were leveled at Beth Beloud.

"Hey!" snarled Dall Stockton, cocking his .30-30. "What—"

"Hands up, both of yuh!" snapped the Coffin 13 boss, his gold-capped teeth glinting as he spoke around his Cuban cigar. "One booger move and I shoot the girl."

Beth went chalk-white as she saw Jepp Vozar jerk the hatchets out of Wing Sing's scrawny fists, then relieve Dall Stockton of his Winchester and holstered Colt.

"Come in." Postell grinned, backing through the door. "we won't keep yuh long, Miss Beloud."

The three Rafter B riders stepped into the Wineglass living room. Flames from a rock fireplace put their shuttering crimson glow over the cobwebby room, which had a fusty smell from long disuse. Beth gave a low gasp as she caught sight of her ex-fiancé, Leon Hesterling, sitting in a split-pole chair beside a table in front of the fireplace. Hesterling was tied hand and foot to the chair with rawhide lass'-rope.

"Thanks, Beth," the remittance man said, and grinned.

"Postell was set to take my scalp if yuh hadn't shown up."

Vozar spoke up from the doorway. "The sheriff's comin' up with the mule string, boss. Think yuh can handle these buskies?"

Grote Postell leaned against the fireplace mantel, his guns trained on Beth Beloud. Without glancing at his foreman, the Coffin 13 boss grated:

"After yuh've unloaded the freight, come on back, Jepp. Bring Drumm with yuh."

Vozar ducked out into the night to carry out his orders. Beth remained staring at the trussed-up figure of Leon Hesterling. On the table in front of the prisoner was a legal document, a bottle of ink and a pen.

"What is this, Duke?" demanded Dall Stockton, glowering at Hesterling with raw suspicion in his eyes. "You bait for a trap, or are yuh wearin' Postell's collar like I've always thought?"

Hesterling lowered his eyes before Stockton's diatribe.

"It's like this, Beth," he said meekly, in the crisp British accents he always used in speaking to her. "Postell doesn't know that you and I split up. He's using me to force you to sign this deed to the Rafter B. Once the ranch has been turned over to the Coffin Thirteen, he's promised to turn us loose. If you don't sign, he'll kill you and Stockton and Wing sing as well. That's how it stacks up."

Beth sagged into a chair, Stockton and the Chinese standing behind her. Neither of her loyal Rafter B friends dared make a hostile move, knowing that Postell's first bullet would snuff out the girl's life.

"Don't sign that deed, Beth!" Dall Stockton panted in her ear. "If Hesterling ain't double-crossin' yuh, then Postell will kill him along with us. Signin' the deed won't turn us loose."

Hesterling writhed frantically in his bonds. Over by the fireplace, Grote Postell toyed with is six-guns, grinning maliciously.

"Think it over, Beth," the Coffin 13 boss said. "We've

got lots of time. Is Hesterling's life worth the Rafter B to yuh?"

Beth buried her face in her hands, unable to arrive at any definite conclusion about her former fiancé. If Hesterling was working for the Coffin 13 secretly, then that explained why he had urged her to sell to Grote Postell during the time that had elapsed since her father's death. If so, his life was not worth saving, at Postell's terms.

Fifteen minutes elapsed, during which the girl showed no signs of having come to a decision. Grote Postell showed no hint of impatience, enjoying this supenseful delay as a cat enjoys playing with a helpless mouse.

Hesterling was fidgeting in his bonds, pleading with the girl in the name of their former association to save his life, assuring her that he was guiltless of any complicity with Grote Postell in this set-up.

Finally the tension was broken by the return of Jepp Vozar. Postell glanced around at his foreman.

"Sheriff with yuh?" he demanded.

Vozar grinned venomously. "He stayed down at the warehouse with the freight, Boss."

Vozar stepped over to the table and glanced at the still unsigned deed to the Rafter B.

"What's the matter? Won't she put her John Henry on that paper, boss?"

Dall Stockton spoke up explosively. "No, and she ain't goin' to sign it! Yuh can go to—"

Vozar snapped a six-gun from holster and, stepping around the table, thrust the muzzle against Leon Hesterling's sweat-damp forehead. Turning his snakish eyes on Beth Beloud, Vozar sawed out:

"If yuh ain't signed that deed in five ticks of the clock, I'll blow the Duke's brains from here to breakfast!"

Beth Beloud came to her feet, shaking off Dall Stockton's outreaching hands.

"I'll sign it!" she screamed. "I—I can't just sit by and see Leon killed!"

Hesterling's cheeks ballooned with relief as he saw Beth dip the pen in ink and scribble her name on the deed. With that signature went all her rights to the legacy old Captain Bob Beloud had left her.

Vozar laughed harshly, withdrawing his gun from Hesterling's head. He picked up the deed, fanned it to dry the ink.

"Hesterling will do to ride the river with, boss," he said. "He pulled the trigger that got rid of old Bob beloud. Now he's made the girl come across with Rafter B!"

A scream escaped Beth's lips as her dazed brain caught the full implication of Vozar's words. She turned toward Lèon Hesterling in disbelief, only to see a surly grin lighting his features.

"Yeah, Beth," her ex-fiancé confessed glibly. "I bushwhacked your dad. You see, the Rafter B owns Lavarock Canyon, and that's the Tombstone Trail's key point in Postell's and my smuggling trade. We had to own the Rafter B, even if I had to marry you to get it."

Beth swayed as if about to faint. Turning, she staggered over to where Dall Stockton waited with open arms to fold her in his embrace.

"It's all right, honey," the redhead said grimly. "They would have killed us anyway. I'm just glad I'm here to be with yuh tonight."

Grote Postell swung his guns to cover the embracing couple. Beth was sobbing bitterly, her head on Stockton's shoulder. To one side, Wing Sing was fingering his black queue and muttering prayers to Buddha, knowing that his own end was not far off.

"Untie the Duke, Vozar!" Postell rasped. "We'll get this nasty business over with fast."

Vozar was reaching for Hesterling's bonds when he was arrested by the sound of a boot kicking open the front door behind him. The half-breed spun around, jerking a gun from holster as he caught sight of the man he knew as Jim Field standing on the threshold.

Flame spat from Hatfield's left-hand gun, and a bullet sped its sightless track past Stockton and Beth, to drill Vozar between the eyes. The *mestizo* foreman pitched face-foremost across Leon Hesterling's lap, triggering his .45 at the floor.

"Drop yore hoglegs, Postell!" Jim Hatfield lashed out, thumbing his right-hand gun to full cock as it covered the Coffin 13 boss. "Yuh're under arrest!"

Postell's Colts dropped with a clatter to the hearthstone as he groped his arms aloft. Firelight gleamed on something shiny pinned to the Lone Wolf's shirt as he stepped into the room. Grote Postell groaned with horror as he recognized the emblem of the Texas Rangers!

Things happened fast then. Dall Stockton released Beth and pounced to snatch up Postell's fallen guns, jabbing their muzzles into the Tombstone Trail chief's middle. Over by the table, Jepp Vozar's corpse thudded to the floor as Leon Hesterling strained against the bonds which held him to the chair. In the Red Duke's eyes was the look of a trapped wolf. Hangrope loomed ahead of him for the self-confessed murder of Beth's father.

"We'll leave yuh tied for the time bein', Hesterling!" Jim Hatfield snapped. "Yore sheriff pard is down at the warehouse, but he's not keepin' guard on the contraband yuh got in Lavarock Canyon this mornin'. He's dead. Vozar knifed him."

Hesterling made a cawing sound in his throat. Hatfield picked up the deed which bore Beth Beloud's signature and tossed it into the fireplace, where it went up in smoke.

Seeing that Beth was staring at the law badge on his shirt, Hatfield laughed softly, amused by her confusion.

"I'm not Les Radley, ma'am," he said. "Jim Hatfield's the name. Yuh got me mixed up that night of the stagecoach accident, and since I was travelin' incognito, I didn't let yuh in on my secret. But it looks like we've reached the end of the Tombstone Trail. I've got enough evidence on Grote Postell as leader of the smugglin' bunch to hang him a dozen times."

Postell, realizing that his case was hopeless, puffed on his cigar and tried to ignore the guns which Dall Stockton kept reamed into the lapel of his fustian coat. His gooseberry eyes followed Jim Hatfield as the Texas Ranger stepped over to the table, picked up the ink-wet pen, and scribbled something on the back of a sheet he ripped from an ancient calendar.

"A telegram to my Ranger boss over in Austin, Roaring Bill McDowell," the Lone Wolf said. "You may be interested in what I'm reporting to Ranger headquarters, Postell. It goes like this: 'Tombstone Trail case finished. Leader is Grote Postell, prominent Thundergust Basin cattlemen and Alto saloon owner. Have him in custody along with accomplice named Leon Hesterling. Have located warehouse full of contraband. Les Radley still at large as I explained in my last telegram relayed from Presidio this week. Signed, Jim Hatfield.' "

CHAPTER XX

Trail's End

Quiet and smiling Hatfield folded the telegram and handed it to Beth Beloud's Chinese cook, who was grinning from ear to ear.

"Yuh're the only man we can spare," he told Wing Sing. "I want yuh to ride to Alto and get the Overland Telegraph operator to put this on the wires tonight, savvy? Bill McDowell will be glad to know this case is sewed up."

Wing Sing thrust the message inside his blouse and bowed.

"Will do," he sing-songed. "Velly good chore for China boy."

Hatfield glanced around the room.

"I'll go out to the barn and bring hosses," he said to Stockton. "Ride herd on Postell and Hesterling while I'm gone."

Dall Stockton laughed harshly.

"With pleasure, Hatfield!" he said. "There's nothing

I'd rather do than burn a couple of caps on these pole-cats, but if you want 'em to hang legal, I'll close-hobble my trigger fingers."

Jim Hatfield and Wing Sing left the Wineglass living room then. After a short interval, those left there heard a thud of hoofbeats as the Chinese sped away from the homestead, bound for Alto with the Ranger's telegraph message.

Boots thudded on the porch outside and Beth turned expectantly, believing that the Texas Ranger was returning.

It came as a grim shock to the girl when the door slammed open and she found herself staring at the red-rimmed eyes of the man who had been Jim Hatfield's prisoner aboard the Wells-Fargo stage an eternity ago—the outlaw she now knew was the real Les Radley.

Radley was ignoring the girl, as he leveled the guns he had stolen from Jim Hatfield across the room at Dall Stockton.

"Drop the hardware, son!" the Tombstone Trail outlaw rasped, clicking his guns to full cock. "What goes on here, Postell?"

Despair clawed at Dall Stockton as he saw death staring at him from the black bores of the guns held by this stranger. An instant later Grote Postell had jerked the six-guns from the Rafter B ramrod's hands—and the tables were turned with a rapidity that left Stockton gasping.

"Good work, Radley!" Postell panted shakily. "Where'd you turn up from?"

Radley stepped across the room to untie Leon Hesterling's ropes, Postell keeping his guns trained on Stockton and the girl.

"I drifted over to the Coffin Thirteen tonight and the roustabout said yuh was out," Radley explained. "I saw yuh leave Alto this afternoon, so I lit a shuck for the Wineglass, figgerin' yuh'd be here at headquarters. Lucky I got here when I did, eh?"

Leon Hesterling came to his feet, and, reaching out,

seized Beth by the arm and hurled her roughly into the chair he had just vacated.

"I can't shoot a woman," the Red Duke grated, as he started tying the girl to the chair with the ropes recently removed from his own body by Les Radley. "But Postell and I have got to head for Mexico, because it's too late to head off Wing Sing and intercept that telegram to Ranger headquarters. Maybe, if somebody gets close enough to hear you screamin', you'll be rescued before you starve, Beth. It's the best I can do for you."

Les Radley headed for the front door.

"Jim Hatfield's down at the barn," he said. "He's the meat I'm after. I'll go down and cash in that Ranger's chips for him."

Postell, his guns in Stockton's spine, nodded grimly. "*Bueno.* We'll come along as soon as the Duke finishes hogtyin' the girl." Postell grinned bleakly. "Even with Jim Hatfield dead, he's won out. That telegram busts up our smugglin' ring and runs us out of Texas for keeps."

Les Radley headed out into the darkness, triumph welling through him. A lantern glowed out in the Wineglass barn, where the Lone Wolf, suspecting no trouble, was busy saddling horses for his prisoners.

Revenge would be sweet tonight, Radley thought, coming at the very climax of what Jim Hatfield probably regarded as the most hard-won case of his adventurous career. It would be a pleasure to blast the Lone Wolf into eternity while the taste of victory was still sweet on his lips.

Guns in hand, Les Radley reached the barn, approaching the ramshackle building with great stealth. He peeped through a knothole in the wall to size up the lay of things before he made his play. Texas Ranger Jim Hatfield, humming a tune by lantern-light, was busy putting saddles aboard Vozar's and Postell's cow ponies.

Stepping to the barn door, Radley let a jingle of his spurs betray his approach. Hatfield, both hands filled with a stock saddle he was carrying, whirled about—

and froze stockstill as he saw the fugitive Radley stalking toward him behind leveled guns.

Killing lust had come to a boil in the outlaw's face as he saw the horror and despair which crossed Hatfield's face. Gun expert that he was, the Ranger could not possibly drop the saddle and make his draw in the face of this point-blank drop.

"Looks like trail's end for you, *Lobo Solo!*" jeered the outlaw. "I got Postell and the Red Duke out of yore little trap. It looks like yore plans went sour all along the line."

A crunch of straw behind him startled Radley then, but he relaxed instantly, knowing that either Postell or Hesterling had come down to the barn to back him in case he ran into trouble in his showdown with Jim Hatfield.

But the voice which issued from the shadows at his back was a woman's voice, the voice of Zolanda Ruiz:

"I've been trailing you ever since you left me in Alto, Les. I had to make sure of my target."

Radley spun around, in time to see flame spit from the bore of the derringer which Zolanda held in her fist. The bullet smashed Radley below the heart, dumping him to his knees. With superhuman effort he managed to lift his guns and both Colts blasted at the same instant.

Zolanda was still standing there at the far range of the lantern's glow, a taut smile on her lips, as death glazed her husband's eyes and he slumped backward on the reasty straw which carpeted the barn floor.

Jim Hatfield dropped his saddle and strode forward, stepping over Les Radley's corpse. Zolanda lowered her smoking gun and took a faltering step forward.

"You saved my life, Zolanda!" panted the Ranger. "Now, if I can get back to the ranchhouse in time, I'll try to save Dall Stockton from those—"

Without a sound, Zolanda Ruiz crumbled in her tracks, and for the first time Hatfield realized that the front of her dress was soaked with blood, which blended with the scarlet fabric.

Seizing her in his arms, he saw twin bullet-holes

punched through her dress just below the neckline. Radley's shots had struck home, even when the outlaw was dead on his feet.

"I—I love you, Senor Jeem," came a rattly whisper from the Mexican woman's throat. "*Vaya con Dios.*"

Her head fell back, and Hatfield felt his throat constrict as he realized that Zolanda had rescued him from doom at the cost of her own life.

He heard voices coming from the direction of the ranchhouse then, and he lowered the dead dancing girl gently to the straw and raced over to leap into the shelter of a barn stall, out of the betraying light of the lantern.

"I heard more than one shot!" came Leon Hesterling's voice from just outside the barn door. "Radley must have shot up that Ranger like a sieve. We'll give Dall the same dose."

The Red Duke appeared in the barn doorway then, with Grote Postell and Dall Stockton close behind him. The Coffin 13 boss had a six-gun jammed against the Rafter B waddy's back.

Hesterling had taken three strides into the barn when he caught sight of Zolanda Ruiz' corpse sprawled there. Five feet further on was another human shape, clad in batwing chaps and a faded linsey-woolsey shirt.

Hesterling's mouth worked like a fish's for seconds before a sound issued from his throat. Pointing a long finger at the dead man sprawled there, the Duke choked out:

"That—that ain't the Ranger! It's Radley!"

Dall Stockton flung himself face downward on the floor of the barn at that instant, seizing the opportunity which Grote Postell's pertrified amazement granted him.

Before Postell could lower his gun and pull trigger, Jim Hatfield's icy voice issued from a nearby stall:

"Yore target's over here, Postell!"

Postell and Hesterling whirled as one toward the sound of that keening voice. They saw the lantern's glow strike the circled star of the Lone Wolf's law badge, as Jim Hatfield moved out of cover behind V-spread six-guns.

With a squall of defiance, Grote Postell snapped gun-hammer. The bullet smashed slivers from the frame of the manger behind Jim Hatfield, tearing a slot through the Ranger's chap wings.

The leader of the Tombstone Trail smugglers didn't get a chance to correct his aim with a second shot. The big Colts bucked and roared in Hatfield's grasp, and bullet-holes appeared an inch apart in Postell's beetling forehead.

Hesterling screamed his teror and fled through the barn door even as Postell toppled forward. The Coffin 13 boss had hardly struck the dirt before Dall Stockton had clawed the gun from his fist and leaped to the door-way in pursuit of the Red Duke.

Jim Hatfield heard Stockton's gun make its harsh breach of the night's stillness, heard the clatter of Leon Hesterling's running boots suddenly halt, out across the yard.

Dall Stockton turned back into the barn, his freckled face beaming in the lantern shine.

"If yuh'll excuse me, Hatfield," chuckled the Rafter B foreman, "I got to get up to the house and untie my future bride. Just as Postell led me out of there, I told her I'd be back to propose, like I should of done years ago. And Beth said she would accept me, by gum!"

Hatfield felt the tension run out of his body then. "Run along, son." He grinned. "Good luck to yuh both."

Dall Stockton sprinted off through the night, toward the lighted doorway of the Wineglass homestead shack where Postell and Hesterling had left the girl to face death by slow starvation. Her reunion with the man who loved her belonged to her alone. The Ranger curbed an impulse to walk over to the house and congratulate them.

The moon lifted its curved sickle horns over the distant Rosillos at that moment, bathing the homestead and the rugged Corazones with its argent witch glow. Crickets trilled in the roundabout shadows; a gentle breeze swept off Thundergust Basin, bringing the spicy scent of sage and cactus blossoms to Hatfield's nostrils.

It pleased him to know that the Rafter B was forever free of the Coffin 13's expanding empire after tonight.

Hesterling lay sprawled beside the horse corral fifty yards away, dropped by Stockton's bullet. In the remote distance, the lights of Alto twinkled and pulsed through the Texas night, reminding the Ranger of Wing Sing and the telegram which he would dispatch to Roaring Bill McDowell.

"Looks like I was too optimistic in my report," mused the Lone Wolf. "Here the Tombstone Trail case is history, and I don't have a single prisoner to show for my trouble!"

He headed off into the moonlight to get Goldy. They would be hitting the trail for Austin in the morning.

TO THE READER

If you enjoyed this book, you will be glad to know that there are many others just as well written, just as interesting, to be had in the Fiction House Press Library.

You will find the Fiction House Press Library online at

www.FictionHousePress.com

www.ingramcontent.com/pod-product-compliance
Lightning Source LLC
LaVergne TN
LVHW091007080826
845145LV00003B/1158